# HOW TO CATCH A PRINCE

## CHESTER FALLS BOOK 1

### ANA ASHLEY

Cover design: Rhys, Ethereal Design

Editor: Victoria Milne

Join Ana's Facebook Group Café RoMMance for exclusive content,
and to learn more about her latest books at anawritesmm.com!

*To everyone that has been on the other end of me moaning, crying, despairing, laughing, hoping, working, dreaming.*
*To those close friends... cough... Rhys... who have been there for the above and more.*
*Your friendship and support means more than you'll ever know.*

*Ana*

*x*

# 1

## KRIS

I PACED the length of the music room, my dress shoes making far too much noise on the wooden floor. The faces of my ancestors looked down at me from their portraits.

I admired the image of my paternal grandfather. I'd been told I looked just like him ever since I'd learned to recognize his face from the dozens lining the room, but he'd been a ruler, a king, something I hopefully would never be.

This room was my favorite, as it had been his. The grand piano, positioned so I could look out into the grounds of the palace when I played, was my escape from the expectations that came with being second in line for the throne of one of Europe's smallest, but richest, monarchies.

The door on the far side of the room opened. I didn't have to turn around to know who was coming in. The familiar click-clack of my older sister's heels gave it away. "Kristof, what have you done this time?"

At only five foot five and with the skin and face of a porcelain doll, Aleksandra looked delicate, almost breakable. She was often underestimated, a mistake many had made, because once Aleksandra spoke, anyone in her presence would not dare doubt why she would one day be the reigning queen of Lydovia, a small European country sandwiched between Greece and Bulgaria.

"Would you believe me if I said it wasn't me?"

Aleksandra gave me a poised stare and sat down graciously on one of the sofas adorning the room.

"Kris," she said, her voice softening, bringing back the sister I'd been so close to growing up we may as well have been twins. "I've seen the papers, so I know what the press thinks. Why don't you tell me what really happened?"

"I've done a lot of things I'm not proud of in my twenty-nine years, but you know I've never done drugs." In fact, I rarely did any of the things I was accused of doing by the press.

"Sergei?" Aleks asked.

"What do you think?"

"I'm going to fucking kill him."

I laughed at my sister's outburst. I sat next to her on the sofa and pulled her into my arms. The moments when we could be just brother and sister and talk with no one listening were becoming rarer since our father had expressed his wish to abdicate the throne as soon as Aleksandra married.

"I'm going to miss this, big sis."

"Me too, Brat. Me too." She sighed. Aleks calling me by my childhood nickname made me feel at home like few things did these days.

Despite Lydovia's geographical position, it had adopted English as the official language more than a century ago when a Lydovian princess married into the British royal family.

Most Lydovians were also fluent in Greek and Bulgarian. As a child, Aleks had adopted the Bulgarian word for brother, *brat,* as my nickname because she thought it was funny, and it had stuck.

"How's Phillip?" I asked.

Aleks's expression softened even further at the mention of her husband-to-be. "Do you remember when we were twelve and ran away because we didn't want to be royal anymore?"

I laughed because I did remember. Phillip was the son of distant cousins who, although not in direct line to the throne, were close to the king and queen. Sergei, on the other hand, was the son of our nanny. We'd all grown up together, running around the grounds of the palace like it was our own playground. For Aleks and I, the palace was more like a prison, and we'd desperately wanted to know what it was like on the other side of the walls. We'd wanted unsupervised access to the people of our country, so at Aleks's demand, we'd decided to run away and had nearly gone through with it until Phillip had intervened.

"He was looking out for you even then." My chest tightened. I wanted to make my father and our people proud. I also wanted to find the one person that could be to me what Phillip was to Aleks, the matching half of my heart that would stop me from jumping the wall.

The problem was that my best-friend-turned-boyfriend, well, ex-boyfriend, was causing all sorts of trouble.

"Why is Sergei doing this?" Aleks asked.

"He's hurt since we broke up last month."

Aleksandra got up from the sofa and walked toward the door leading to the terrace and the gardens beyond.

"Come for a walk with me," she said.

The snow-capped mountains in the distance were

in contrast to the bright wildflowers and green grass of the palace gardens. Two opposites that were in perfect harmony. I often felt I was like the mountains and the flowers, winter and spring. But unlike the landscape of my country, I hadn't yet found that same synergy between the prince and the man.

Aleks wrapped her arm around me as we walked side by side toward the lake at the bottom of the gardens. I respected and admired my sister more than anyone else in the world, our father included. That said a lot because I'd always had a great relationship with the king, especially after my mother had passed away due to an undiagnosed heart condition when we were still children.

"You know this can't carry on, Kris. I know you prefer to keep your work to yourself, but you need to give the press something positive to talk about."

I sighed. I knew my sister was right. The reason I'd resisted so far was because the people I helped didn't deserve to be brought into the ugly limelight of click-bait journalism.

No one wanted to know that Prince Kristof of Lydovia worked as a business consultant for a number of charities to make sure they were able to continue helping people. No one wanted to know how many hours I spent with kids on the soccer fields, training them and patching up those bruised knees and egos.

I knew the press would twist it and find some way to turn my uninteresting desk job into a sensationalist headline.

"These are people's lives we're talking about, Aleks. I will speak to Sergei."

"This isn't just about Sergei, and you know it. We didn't choose to be in the position we're in. We were born into it, which comes with a lot of privilege but also with a reality most people never have to face."

"I'm sorry. I know this isn't easy on you, either. I'll do better, and I'll sort things out with Sergei, okay?"

I gave my sister a kiss and held her in a tight hug. "You're going to be a great queen."

"Damn right I am."

We both laughed, but I didn't miss how Aleks's posture changed. I knew what that meant, but there was nothing I would refuse my sister, so I prepared myself for the incoming request.

"I need you to attend the president's annual ball in Washington."

I stared at Aleks, trying to see if she was playing a joke on me. It wasn't her style, but then again, I knew she was quite annoyed that my name was once again in the press for the wrong reasons.

Her expression remained unchanged. No, not unchanged. She'd put on her "I'm talking to you as future queen" face.

It had been four years since Lydovia had had any kind of representation from the royal family at the President of the United States' annual ball. Of course, since the newly elected president had reintroduced more inclusive laws and was openly supportive of LGBTQ people, sending a representative from our country was a show of alliance and would re-establish the good relationship we'd always had with the country.

"Why me?" It didn't make sense that Aleks or our father would want me to go, considering the press kept asking for a statement on what had happened at the club. I took a step toward a statue that faced the small lake and leaned against it, facing away from my sister.

"See it as an opportunity to show our people that you can be a good representative of the royal family."

"I *am* a good representative of the royal family, Aleks. Do you not see all the work..." I ran my fingers through my hair, hoping the move would help calm me down.

"Brat."

I knew it was pointless arguing with Aleks, so I accepted my fate.

"I'd be happy to attend the ball," I said.

Aleks nodded, a tight smile arising as she started walking toward the palace.

"What else is there?" I saw the apology in her eyes and moved to fall into step with her. "Are you going to ask me to also go into hiding until this press thing goes away before I attend the ball? You know I don't have the hair to pull off a good Rapunzel."

She gazed down for a brief moment as if she was searching for the right thing to say.

"Are you serious?"

"We need to manage this, and I think it would be good if your name wasn't printed on the headline of every newspaper for a while." Aleks took a deep breath and clasped her hands. "Why don't you fly to the States and stay somewhere discreet until the ball? Use that time to think about what you want to do when you come back."

It wasn't a request, and I knew it, but maybe it was just what I needed.

"I suppose I need to speak to the king about this," I said with resignation.

"He wasn't the one who called you here today. I was."

I shouldn't have been surprised that once again my sister had come to my rescue, and like a true leader, she'd known exactly how to exercise her power. I knew the same conversation with the king would have resulted in a different outcome, one less pleasant than spending a few weeks in some American hideaway where no one would know who I was.

"Oh, and you should speak to Mimi," Aleks said, a small smile gracing her lips.

"She's here?"

I didn't wait for an answer before running back up the steps to the terrace in search of the woman who'd been there for me since I was born and whose arms I'd cried into when I'd lost my mother.

As I turned into the main corridor leading to a number of function rooms, I walked past a very irritated head chef, which meant only one thing, Mimi was in the kitchen. During the time Mimi had lived at the palace, her place to relax and wind down had been the kitchen. She'd loved to cook, bake, and create almost as much as she'd loved her job as the royal nanny.

"Mimi?" I called from the kitchen door, reluctant to go all the way in.

"In here, darling." She was halfway inside a cupboard, no doubt looking for the only cake tin that would yield the perfect cake or something equally as ridiculous.

"You know we have people that can do that for you."

Her head came out from inside the cupboard so quickly I wondered how she hadn't bumped her head.

"Kristof Ivan Maxim, have you learned nothing from me?"

"'God gave me two perfect hands. I can use them as well as the next person.'" I repeated the lesson my nanny had drilled into me since I was a child so I wouldn't forget that the title was an addition to the person and *not* the other way around.

"Can I give my nanny a hug?" I said, pulling her up by her hand and lifting her in a hug that raised her feet off the floor.

As soon as I put Mimi down, she scanned me from top to bottom before she took a deep breath. I held her hand up to my lips, placed a soft kiss, and guided her to the table where there was a fresh pot of coffee and china laid out on a tray. No doubt the chef had been in the process of preparing the king's after-noon coffee before Mimi had unceremoniously kicked him out of his kitchen. That meant our time alone would come to an end shortly.

"Kristof," she said, her voice full of worry, "the papers are saying horrendous things about you and Sergei. Is it true?"

"Sergei and I broke up last month. I haven't seen him since. I guess this is his way of showing he's hurting, or that he's really angry with me."

Mimi looked surprised. "Why did you break up? You've been together since you were teenagers."

I took a deep breath. "I love him, he was…is my best friend. But I am not *in* love with him."

If I was honest, I'd say I hadn't been in love with Sergei for a while. Sergei had been my best friend for as long as I could remember. We'd been each other's first kiss at the tender age of fourteen, followed by all the other firsts. In the safety of the palace and away from the eyes of the press, we'd explored our sexuality, fallen in love, and grown into the men we were today.

Even when Sergei had left to start his career in the royal army, we'd managed to stay together. At the time, I'd hoped Sergei would move into the palace permanently in-between the times he needed to be abroad serving in the name of our king.

Sergei was the safe option. He'd been around the

royal family long enough to know the protocol. He would fill the shoes of the royal prince's husband perfectly, and that was the problem.

In the last year, the thrill I'd felt being with Sergei when we were young wasn't there anymore, and, quite selfishly, I wanted more. I wanted the love I'd seen between my parents, the love I saw between my sister and Phillip. All-consuming, never fading, once-in-a-lifetime kind of love.

I took a deep breath and then let it out slowly. "I'm going to be away for a while. I need to speak to Sergei, but he's not answering my calls."

Mimi looked sad but resigned.

"I will see what I can do, my dear."

"Thank you, Mimi."

I looked at my beloved nanny. She'd never taken sides between me and Sergei. Not that I'd blame her if she did, after all, Sergei was her son and only blood relative. A pang of sadness hit me.

## 2

## CHARLIE

I LOOKED at my wristwatch and sighed. It was nearly six o'clock. I should have finished my shift at four.

The mild weather always increased footfall in the menswear department at Clarence's, but in the last few weeks, it seemed every man in the city had run out of clothes. Which was why I'd stayed on to help my team with a delivery that had arrived later than expected.

Another hour of checking emails and speaking to some of the team, and I'd finally be able to head home to pack for my week-long vacation.

I'd been looking forward to my sister Hannah's wedding since she'd announced the engagement to her girlfriend, Ellie.

I hadn't had proper time off from work in

months, so the wedding, apart from giving me the rare opportunity to spend some quality time with my family, was also a much-needed break.

"Charlie, can I have a word?" my manager, Frasier, asked, walking into the stockroom.

"Sure."

"Holly in Fragrances called in sick. She's going to be off for a week. Would you be able to come in this weekend to cover her department?"

I tried to keep my face neutral, which was a miracle of nature considering inside my blood was boiling. Not only had I overheard a conversation between Holly and a colleague about calling in sick to go to Cape Cod with her boyfriend but my vacation had been booked for months, for goodness sake.

"I'm afraid I can't, Frasier. It's my sister's wedding, so I'm going to be off for the next week."

Frasier's eyes bulged. "Who authorized this vacation?"

"You did. Months ago."

I enjoyed working with Frasier when it was us against the world on the store floor, serving customers and managing the team. But when Frasier went into manager mode, he was a downright jerk, no two ways about it.

"Do you need a whole week? Isn't the wedding just a day?"

"Well, yes, but…" I tried to remember if the train ticket I'd booked could be amended. I hated the pressure to say yes all the time, and sometimes it felt that I did it a lot more than any of my other colleagues who seemed to be picked for certain projects or for promotion.

"I'll check if I can change my train ticket." I relented. "I may be able to come back a few days earlier." I hated seeing the small smirk of victory on Frasier's lips.

"That's good. You know the management team is keeping an eye on you for the next sales manager vacancy. These things all count."

I prayed to my fairy godmother that the train ticket couldn't be amended so I had a genuine reason and evidence to justify being away for the whole week. This was the one vacation I'd booked months ago and was more than entitled to take.

Another two hours later and only minutes short of the store's closing time, I was finally on my way home. As soon as I was able to claim a seat on the bus, I took my sketchpad out of my bag. I'd seen two teenagers at the bus stop reading from the same book. The image was stuck in my head because unlike most people at the bus stop, the two kids weren't on their cellphones. I wondered what kind of book it was and smiled to myself, knowing that just like those teenagers, when a book really gripped me, I couldn't put it down.

Despite the bumpy bus ride, as soon as my pencil touched the paper, I felt myself relax and finally wind down from the long busy day at work. My favorite sound in the world was the scratching of graphite on paper, and even with the noise of the bus, I knew it so well it was as though I could hear it as I sketched the outline of the two teenagers.

"Some people don't know how fortunate they're born."

I looked at the old lady sitting next to me reading one of those gossip magazines. She shook her head and huffed, muttering something to herself. I went back to my sketch, where I was now drawing the book so the shape between the two figures was a heart. Maybe I could draw the same picture but with two girls and gift it to my sister after the wedding; after all, Hannah and Ellie had fallen in love at Book-marked, the bookstore in Chester Falls, our hometown.

"Look at this." The lady nudged me and showed me the magazine. "We work our whole lives and can't even get discounted bus passes, and these princes squander it all away on drugs. Shameful."

I wasn't sure what the lady expected me to say, but the headline caught my eye. *Tension in the Lydovian Royal Family: Prince Kristof caught in drug-fueled party.* Beneath the headline, there was a photo of a few people partying in a dark club. From the angle the photo was taken, the man couldn't be identified, but he looked to be in his late twenties, maybe early thirties. I didn't bother reading the rest of the article. I gave the lady a smile, pretending to agree with her, and put my sketchpad back in my bag. My stop was coming up and I didn't care much for whatever European royal prince was doing with his money and time. Besides, I had bigger things to worry about such as what to pack for the wedding.

---

"Coffee, tea, or cocktail?" Tom, my roommate, called out from the kitchen.

"Definitely cocktail. And while you're at it, can I have some fairy dust and rainbow sprinkles to transform my wardrobe into something decent?" That last bit was muttered more to myself than my roommate.

Tom came into my room minutes later with two

cocktails in hand. "One cranberry hippo kiss coming right up."

"Cranberry hippo kiss?"

"Because when you've had one too many, you won't care if the guy kisses like a hippo. Wet and sloppy."

"Your cocktails are non-alcoholic," I pointed out.

"It's the sugar, honey. It'll make you happy. Now, what did you say about sprinkles?"

"Never mind." I sighed.

"What's the matter, honeybun?"

I sat on the edge of my single bed and took a sip of the cocktail, letting the fruity sweet flavor tease my taste buds before I confessed. "I have nothing to wear."

Tom looked around the room and laughed. "Darling, you have more clothes here than we have in our warehouse at work."

"Yes, but these are work clothes," I said, leaning against the headboard. I stared at Tom, who was definitely the more fashion-savvy of the two of us, and he had already started pulling clothes from the closet and was holding them up for inspection.

When I'd started my job as a Christmas temp at Clarence's, Tom had taken the time to teach me the ropes. A temp job had become permanent, and after

I'd finished my art degree from the Massachusetts School of Art and Design with no prospects of a real paying job doing what I loved the most, I'd accepted a promotion to sales supervisor alongside my best friend.

"What are you talking about? You have some great stuff here," Tom said. "Worry not, my friend. There's a reason why you keep me around."

"What's that?"

"I'm super fabulous, and I'm going to fabulize the shit out of your wardrobe." I trusted Tom's fashion expertise, but in reality, we had different styles. Tom was like a pixie on crack distributing happy rainbow dust to everyone around him; I was more of a T-shirt and jeans kind of guy. Tom was bright colors and exotic fruit; I was navy blue and steak and fries.

I admired Tom for being so unashamedly colorful. He knew himself and wasn't afraid to be who he was. The only time I felt the same way was when I had my sketchpad and pencil in my hand, but even then, my drawings were all shades of the same gray color.

Tom put aside various combinations of shirts, pants, and, thankfully, some comfortable jeans and T-shirts.

"Here you are," Tom said proudly. "Your vacation

capsule wardrobe that will highlight all your best features, and yes, I mean that ass." Tom winked.

"You have a twitch in your eye," I said.

"Don't mock my lack of sexy winking capability. God had to give me one flaw. Anyways," Tom said, drawing out the *a* as he sat next to me on the bed and took the last sip of his cranberry hippo kiss. "What have you got planned for the week?"

"I think there's a family barbecue, the rehearsal dinner, and then the wedding day. Most of the time I'll be hanging out with my family, I guess," I said without taking my eyes off the bottom of the cocktail glass.

"You don't sound enthused."

I pulled my knees up to my chest and rested my head on the bed frame, taking a deep sigh.

"You're going to a wedding, not an execution," Tom said, "and even if it was an execution, it wouldn't be yours, so why the long sigh?"

"My ex is going to be there."

And now that I'd said it aloud, my heart rate had picked up its pace, and not in a good way.

"Why is your ex there?"

"Ever heard of the boy who fell in love with his brother's straight best friend?"

"Nooooo." Tom turned around and sat cross-legged in front of me with his head propped on his hands like he was waiting for the scoop of the year. "I have to know this story. You owe me."

"Why?"

"Darling, I've just packed your suitcase for you and made you a cocktail. Start talking."

I groaned.

"It's not that exciting. Long story short, I had a crush on him but thought he was straight. Turns out he wasn't, but he wasn't out, so our relationship became a secret. He broke my heart, but he's still Connor's best friend, so where the family is, he is too. The end."

"Oh, Charlie." Tom sighed.

"Yep."

And that was the sole dark cloud in the blue sky that was seeing my family. I'd always been an open book as far as my family was concerned. They'd even known I was gay before I came out to them.

I still didn't know how they'd never found out Rory and I were together all those years ago. I hadn't liked it one bit, but I'd respected Rory's wishes because I'd been so completely under his spell.

Now? Would I still be able to hide the hurt when in Rory's presence? I wasn't so sure.

I really missed my family and wished I could see

them more, but the thought of bumping into my secret ex still stopped me from getting on the train out of Boston to the small town of Chester Falls, Connecticut.

Tom jumped off the bed and did a twirly dance around himself.

"I have the solution," he sang. "I can come with you and be your fake boyfriend for the weekend. I'll make your ex so jealous that by the time I'm finished with him, he'll be flying out of the closet shitting rainbows and glitter."

I couldn't help but laugh at my friend's crazy solution.

"Thanks, fairy godmother, but first, no one would believe it. Remember, my brother and sister have met you and know we're not together. And second, you're working this weekend."

Tom deflated a little, and I wanted to hug him.

"I'll see if I can find someone to swap."

"No point. Holly is sick," I said, making a double quote gesture with my fingers. "As it is, Frasier already asked me if I could work, so there's no way you can have time off."

"Are you shitting me? You've had this week booked off for ages. He can't make you come in, can he? Why don't you call HR—"

I got up from the bed and put my hands on Tom's gesticulating arms.

"Calm down, superwoman. I've already texted Frasier to tell him I can't change my train ticket. My vacation is going ahead as planned."

It was nice having someone in my corner at work, and I knew that if Tom wasn't there with me, I'd have quit ages ago.

"Well, Tinker Bell, I need to sleep because my train is at stupid o'clock in the morning because I must have been drunk when I booked it." I had been. The thought of seeing Rory made me so anxious, I couldn't even book the train ticket without some liquid courage, hence the reason for the 6:00 a.m. ticket rather than the 6:00 p.m. one.

"Okay, goodnight, sweetie," Tom said before he gave me a hug.

When Tom left the room, I steeled myself for the one thing I needed to do before I could see my family, but when I reached for my cellphone, I realized I'd been beaten to the post.

Rory: *Hey, Charlie, I was wondering if we could talk before you see your family?*

Charlie: *Okay. I'll text you when I get there.*

# 3

## KRIS

I LOOKED at the moving landscape outside the car window. It hadn't changed much since we'd landed at Boston Logan Airport.

We'd left the city; I knew that much because since we'd left the highway, we'd driven through what looked like smaller towns.

For a moment, I wondered if it would have been better to have gone to England instead. There the green rolling fields with patches of trees peppering the boundaries, the small villages with handfuls of cottages and the obligatory church at the end of the road, and the rose bushes and green hedges were so much like Lydovia, I knew I'd have felt more at home.

"Where is this place we're going to?" I asked.

I looked at the man sitting beside me, his eyes focused on the road. James was still tall. Taller than me, which was something considering I was six foot three, but he was no longer the skinny, cute guy I'd met years ago. Far from it. This new James was built like a tank with muscles in all the right places.

Keeping my security team to a single person had been a long argument with my father and sister, but one I'd won in the end.

When I was introduced to the man assigned with keeping me safe, I wouldn't have recognized him if it weren't for the one feature that hadn't changed one bit: his baby face.

James and I had met at college. He'd stood out from the rest of the students because he hadn't worn the right clothes and had kept mostly to himself, but what was special about him was that he didn't rely on his family name to get anywhere. He worked hard for everything he had, from the books he needed to the grades he got.

I, on the other hand, had worked so hard to be invisible that I'd stood out only to one person. The one who, when he'd found out who I was, never stopped treating me like the friend I didn't think I'd need while I was away from home and Sergei.

After Harvard, James had joined the army. I'd

never understood why tall, skinny James Bennett had wanted to go into the army, but he'd just said it was something he had to do.

We'd kept in touch over the years, but he never talked about work or his life. All I knew was that whatever he did, it took him all over the world. That I figured out from the collection of cheesy postcards I'd collected over the years from him.

"We're not far now, sir."

"James, did you or did you not have your tongue down my throat five minutes after we first met and before I even had a chance to tell you I had a boyfriend at the time?" I looked at him and saw a cute blush appear on the tops of his ears.

"Yes…sir, that is er…affirmative."

"For goodness sake, James, there's no one around. Please call me Kris."

"Yes, sir," he replied with a smirk.

True to his word, James turned into a road leading up to what looked like an English manor house at the top of a long driveway. Each side of the driveway was green with low-cut grass, but the lack of trees was disappointing. I loved walking outdoors, so the featureless fields surrounding the house were disheartening to see.

"What is this place?"

"It's um…it's my house."

James's normally steady voice faltered slightly, giving me the sensation this wasn't an easy topic of conversation, so I didn't press for more information. As far as I remembered, James's family was just his mom who lived in Boston, and she certainly didn't have the means to own such a property.

The closer we got to the house, the more I realized how big it was, and also was able to observe the state of disrepair it was in. James pulled the car around the side of the house.

I could already feel the muscles in my legs aching for a stretch with the sound of the gravel as the car came to a halt by a set of double doors. Between the flight and the car journey, I could have done with a good walk.

"James, my love, you're here." A tiny lady in a cream and white uniform, and with a clear Irish accent, came out from inside the house and beelined for James. I smiled at seeing how big burly James was no match for a hug from the much shorter and smaller woman.

"Kris, this is Mary, the superpower who runs this house for me." And then it was my turn to be on the receiving end of a warm hug. "Mary has seen more royalty through these doors than a Hans Christian Andersen fairytale, so to her, you're just Kris.

I chuckled, but in reality, I was relieved. If I was meant to lie low, I wanted the opportunity to be treated like a regular person.

"The phone has been ringing off the hook with the press wanting to interview Prince Kristof. We have declined to make a statement, but you know it's only a matter of time until they come here."

I saw James immediately go into special-agent mode. He looked around as though he was expecting real swarms of photographers and journalists. Not that there was any threat against me. I just didn't want the press to know where I was and come flocking to the area and disrupting local people's lives looking for the latest scoop on the prince of Lydovia.

Frustration rose in my chest. If they bothered to check their "facts" before printing their stories, none of this would be necessary, because for all the stuff that appeared in the press, I led a very boring life, and it wasn't often I allowed myself to act my age and go to a club.

"How did this happen?" James asked. "No one knew we were coming here, Mary."

"I've been asking myself the same question. I can trust all our house staff, and even then, only a few knew the exact identity of our guest. I don't know what to say."

I felt like the proverbial rug had been pulled from under my feet. I was hoping for a peaceful few weeks alone, and now I was likely going to be under virtual house arrest.

"Ah, Master James." A man dressed head to toe in tweed joined us. "How are you, son? And this must be Prince Kristof. Welcome, Your Royal Highness."

"You can call him Kris, otherwise he gets a big head, Rupert," James said as Rupert stretched out his hand to shake mine.

"I have a solution," Rupert said. "There are a number of family-run hotels just as you're approaching the next town. My suggestion is that Kris stays in one of them until we can respond to the press and throw the scent off. He won't be recognized by the locals. Most people around here only care about cows and the price of milk. They don't read those gossip magazines."

James stared at the driveway. His brows were drawn together as he took his cellphone out of his pocket and paused before dialing a number.

"Um hi, it's me," James said before turning away from us. "I need a favor." He moved out of earshot.

James's free hand went up to rub the back of his neck as he heard whatever the caller on the other side said.

He paused again and turned around. He smiled, but it didn't reach his eyes.

"James," I started, but he waved his hand and turned his attention back to the call.

"Thank you. That's really great of him to do that." James looked like he was ending the call, but then said, "Um, no, that was all, thank you. Yeah, that would be good. Bye."

Mary took a deep sigh, and Rupert put his arms around her.

"I know, my darling, we never get him for long," he said.

"I hoped it would be longer this time," Mary replied with resignation.

"Hope the five-minute leg stretch was long enough because we're getting back in the carriage for another couple of hours," James said, joining us. "I found you a new castle."

"Does it come with its own prince?"

James laughed. "Nope, it's too early for pumpkin season."

We said our goodbyes to Mary and Rupert, and I apologized for not staying longer. Despite the brief introduction, I'd liked the couple and was sad to leave them.

Minutes later, we found ourselves back in the car in the direction of the highway. Under normal circumstances, I'd have been restless and frustrated, but I was surprisingly calm. Maybe it was the jetlag. I chuckled.

"What," James said.

"Nothing, just funny that I have no clue where I am or where I'm heading, but the press seems to have no issues finding out."

"Yeah, sorry about that. Mary is lovely but too trusting. I'm pretty sure it was someone in the house that tipped them off. I don't know them all yet, but I'll look into it."

"Want to tell me about it?" I asked.

"Nah, it's a long, boring story."

"Well then, in that case, how about you tell me where you're taking me?"

"We're going home."

The way James said it made me look at him. He was looking forward, focused on driving, but there was something about him I couldn't put my finger on.

Home. Was this the place he grew up in? Did he ever go back, considering his mom was in Boston? I turned my head to look out of the window at the moving landscape.

Home. What did it mean to me? All of my life, home had been the palace, the one place where I could be myself without judgment from others. The place that had seen generations of my ancestors walking those corridors; talking, arguing, laughing, strategizing, and this would continue far into the future.

I didn't realize I'd fallen asleep until I felt a hand on my arm.

"We're here."

"Where's here?"

"Chester Falls, Connecticut."

I got out of the car and stretched, letting out a long yawn. Jetlag was definitely catching up with me.

The brick building in front of us was stunning. It looked like a factory that had been repurposed into apartments. It wasn't quite finished yet because a lot of the windows still had protective plastic sheets covering them.

James stared at the building like he wasn't expecting it to be there.

"Are you okay?" I asked, placing my hand on his shoulder.

"What? Oh yeah…okay."

"Right…well, if this is the place, shall we go in?"

"Yes, let's."

I picked up one of my suitcases, James picked up the other, and we walked the short distance to the entrance of the building. It still looked a little like a construction site with planks of wood making a ramp leading to the main doors that were wide open. Now this was somewhere no one would think to look for the prince of Lydovia. It was perfect.

From the side of the building came a guy carrying a number of rolls of fabric.

"Hey, I hope one of you is James; otherwise, I've got my schedule all messed up," the guy said as he laid the fabric rolls on a plastic sheet just inside the doors.

He had an easy, relaxed smile, which, despite my tiredness, I couldn't help but mirror.

"Hi, I'm Tristan," he said.

"Kris," I said, shaking his hand. "Nice to meet you, and thanks for helping me out."

He indicated for us to follow him inside.

"We're still doing a lot of work before the apartments are ready, but we have a couple that are fully furnished and usable."

Tristan took us up two flights of stairs and then along a corridor to the other end of the building. I noticed some of the original features had been kept intact, such as brickwork and the long lines of light fixtures along the corridor.

"The building is gorgeous. What did it used to be?" I asked.

"A textiles mill," both James and Tristan said at the same time.

"Ah, you're a local man, I take it," Tristan said to James. "I moved to Chester Falls for this job a few months ago. Best decision of my life."

The way Tristan's face lit up made me wonder if he'd found more than a new job in this town.

James's cellphone rang as we got to the apartment, so he excused himself after asking me to meet him back at the car.

It didn't take long to get a tour of the one-bedroom apartment.

"It's very basic, but everything works. I'll be around most of the time, but I also live in town, so if you need anything or there's a problem, call me, and I'll be here in ten minutes."

"How far away is the town?" I asked.

Tristan walked to the balcony in the living room and pointed out the small river that flowed alongside the building.

"That down there is the Chester River, if you walk a mile and a half in that direction, you'll be in town. If you look over from the corner of the balcony, you'll see the town hall clock tower."

"Got it, thanks."

"I think that's everything. You have my number if you need anything." He started walking toward the door before I stopped him.

"Tristan, you didn't ask any questions about me. Why? You could have told me to get a hotel in town. "

He looked at me with that easy, friendly smile.

"I know who you are. I mean, you're like a real-life gay Prince Charming." He chuckled. "But you're also a person, and I'm doing a favor for a friend of a friend. That's all."

I nodded and followed him out.

I found James leaning against the car. He had his arms crossed over his chest and he stared off into the distance in the direction of town.

"There's enough room if you want to stay and don't mind sharing a bed. I'll be the little spoon."

The joke snapped James out of whatever state he was in.

"Thanks, but I should go back. If the press thinks you're at my place, I should be seen there without you." He went around the car to the driver's side door. "I'll come back to get you when it's safe for you to return to my place."

James's car soon disappeared from sight, leaving me wondering why he'd seemed so shaken up as soon as we'd arrived in Chester Falls.

I didn't bother having a second look around the apartment before going straight into the bedroom. It was larger than I'd expected. The king-size bed was covered in a plush throw and decorative pillows and invited me to dive in for a nap.

When I woke up again, it was dark outside. I pulled the cord on the bedside table lamp and the room flooded with warm light.

Maybe tomorrow I could go for a walk by the river and explore, but for tonight, I just needed some food, so I got up from the bed and hoped there was somewhere nearby, perhaps a store or restaurant I could go to for dinner.

Would I be recognized? James hadn't advised me on what to do in this situation, and that made me a little nervous. I picked up my cellphone to call James but noticed it didn't have any available signal, so I placed it back on the bedside table. I was never on my own in public. Even when I went out with friends, there was always a bodyguard in the shadows looking out for me.

I shook my head, thinking of all the times I'd wished for this exact moment when I could pretend to be a normal person. I had my chance now. It was like I'd finally climbed the wall and managed to get to the other side where the regular people lived.

My suitcase was bursting at the seams with a variety of outfits. I opened it and took out my most casual pair of jeans and a T-shirt—the one with the Harvard university logo I'd worn so much that the once deep red was now more a faded pink. Looking at my reflection in the mirror, there was nothing about me that screamed royalty, status, and wealth. Excellent.

I opened the door of my apartment and stepped out, making sure to lock the door, my eyes focused on my hands. Even that small task, and the fact I had to remember to do such a thing, made me feel normal. I was certain I could look after myself without James around.

That was until I turned to leave and tripped on a

small suitcase someone had left behind, right by my door.

"Oooh shit." The high pitch of my scream sounded foreign, even to my ears, as my body went down, but before I hit the floor, I was able to grab onto something to stop myself from falling all the way. The only problem was, the *something* was actually a *someone* who I'd dragged down and was now on the floor, on top of me.

# 4

## CHARLIE

WHEN I'D THOUGHT my day couldn't get any worse, I'd clearly underestimated the power of karma, god, the tooth fairy, or whatever it was that was hell-bent on screwing me over.

I'd forgotten to set my alarm the night before and had woken up just in time to get dressed, grab my suitcase, and run for the train, which was about the only thing that had worked out. If it hadn't, I'd have needed to buy a new ticket, which would have cost a fortune.

The first couple of hours of the journey home had been spent answering emails from my team, who had waited until I was off work to request time off, swap shifts, and ask all kinds of questions. Just as I'd replied to one of Frasier's emails about stock availability, my cellphone died. That had been a blessing in disguise. I'd deal with that later.

A technical malfunction with the train had brought the journey to a halt, so I, alongside all the other passengers, had been dropped off at the smallest train station in the whole of Massachusetts and left to wait for the next available train, which had arrived around lunchtime. By then I was bored, tired, and so hungry I'd considered asking my fellow passengers if anyone had any snacks they could spare. Not to mention coffee. Fuck, I'd needed coffee. Like, yesterday.

By midafternoon, I finally arrived at my parent's house where some of my family were also staying for the week.

I hadn't warned anyone I was arriving a few days earlier than expected because I'd wanted to make it a surprise. The first person I bumped into as I opened the door was Aunt Gina.

"Darling, it's been such a long time. Come here," my aunt said while pulling me into a Chanel No. 5 scented hug.

"Hi, Aunt G," I said, hugging her back. "I missed you too. I'll just drop my stuff in my old room and come down to see everyone."

"Yes, honey. They'll be delighted you're early.

They were saying it was such a shame for you to miss the barbecue. Oh, did you know Rory is staying in your room? Apparently, he's having some renovations going on at his place. Hope you don't mind sharing. Oh look, there he is in the kitchen."

I straightened my back as Rory looked in my direction and smiled. He came over and helped me with my suitcase, which was good because I failed to move an inch with the slow realization that I was going to have to share a room with my ex. The ex no one in my family knew was an ex—or gay for that matter.

As soon as we got inside the room, I found myself pinned to the closed door with Rory's mouth on mine. Rory tasted of mint and beer, which was an odd combination, but one I'd been so familiar with when we'd been together. I felt my body responding until my brain caught up and I pushed him away.

"What the fuck, Rory."

"I'm sorry, Charlie. I…you…I couldn't stop myself," Rory said apologetically.

"What are you doing here?" I asked.

Rory's neck reddened as he looked away from me.

"You asked to share my room with me?" My voice had an unattractive pitch, but I didn't care.

"Because I wanted to spend some time with you. I miss you…I miss us."

"No," I said with as much determination as I could muster. "You miss the convenience of being able to jump into bed with me while my family is none the wiser. I'm not a doormat, Rory. Maybe I was innocent once and believed you when you told me you were in love with me. Finding out that you, the person who was meant to love me, were sleeping with other people while I was away at college put things into perspective."

Rory didn't even try to deny it or find some kind of excuse like saying he'd done it because he was angry with me. Not that it would have made a difference because it had hurt all the same. I had, in the five years since, been with other guys, but none had hurt me as much as Rory because I'd been forced to keep everything that happened between us a secret from my family. I'd had to stay away while Rory had kept his place of adoration with my family just because he was my brother's best friend.

I grabbed my suitcase and opened the room door.

"Where are you going?" Rory asked.

"To find another place to stay."

"Where? Don't tell me you're leaving your parents' home for a hotel."

I didn't like the look of defiance and victory in Rory's eyes, so I simply said, "I'll find something."

I only heard Rory behind me saying something along the lines of "you should be so lucky" and "no vacancies" as I dragged my suitcase back to the front door where I bumped into my mom and dad.

My parents couldn't have looked happier to see me, so I agreed to join them for coffee in the lounge. We caught up with news of the wedding activities over the following days as the coffee settled nicely in my stomach, causing me to relax for the first time since I'd woken up that morning.

I still needed to find somewhere to stay, so I told my parents my boyfriend wouldn't be happy knowing I shared a room with another man, albeit a straight one. It was a small lie, but one that would save a lot more questions being raised, even if I left them open-mouthed at the mention of a boyfriend. *Shit.*

After hours of walking around checking the few hotels Chester Falls had to offer, I still hadn't found a place to stay. I hated that Rory had been right; there were no vacancies.

I sat on a bench in the town square considering my lack of options until a familiar face looked over toward me from across the square and then the person waved. I picked up my suitcase and went over to greet my friend and old college roommate, Ben.

Ben had come back to Chester Falls after college to run his aunt's bookstore, Bookmarked, with her. We kept in touch, but since I was rarely in Chester Falls, it had been a while since I'd seen him.

"Well, if it isn't the brother of the bride," Ben said teasingly as he gave me a hug. "It's been a while."

"Believe it or not, it's not the first time I've heard that today," I confessed.

He chuckled. "I can imagine. Come inside, I'm closing for the day shortly. So, what's up? Shouldn't you be home?"

I followed Ben inside Bookmarked. The store had had some updates, but somehow it still smelled as I remembered—paperbacks and something else that was unique and always reminded me of Ben's Aunt Jacqueline.

"Yeah, well my room has been temporarily taken over by Rory, so I haven't got a place to stay."

Ben's eyebrows drew together. "Ellie mentioned something about it, actually. Something about helping out with the wedding?"

It didn't surprise me that Rory had found a plausible excuse, but it still didn't solve my problem.

"Do you know if there are any new hotels out of town I could try?"

At that moment, a car drove around the side of the bookstore, which was not unusual since many locals often used the little spot to park when running errands in town, but it was the way Ben's whole body lit up that told me the person pulling up wasn't just another local.

Ben and I called each other occasionally, and since he was Ellie's best man, we'd caught up recently, which was when he'd told me how he'd met Tristan and Ellie's cunning role in getting them together.

"Man, you're so whipped," I teased.

"With a cherry on top."

As soon as Tristan came in, Ben walked over for a kiss. I had to look away because it felt wrong to watch such an intimate moment. As it was, the way Tristan had looked at Ben when he'd walked into the store was the stuff of fairytales.

"Hi, Charlie, nice to finally meet you," Tristan said without releasing his gentle hold on Ben.

"Babe, would you mind if Charlie crashed upstairs with us?"

"What?" I said. "No, thanks, Ben, but I can look for a hotel. I don't want to be in your way for a whole week."

"If you're looking for a place to stay, I can help," Tristan said.

"Really? You know a hotel nearby?"

"Not quite. We're doing some critical work at the Old Mill this week, so we don't have any appointments for the show homes. You can stay in one of the spare ones."

"Oh my gosh, Tristan, you're a lifesaver." I could have hugged him, but from the way Ben was looking at his boyfriend, I could tell Tristan would be well recompensed for his generosity.

Even as the sky darkened, I could see how much the renovation of the Old Mill had improved the surrounding area. There were benches and grassy areas with wildflowers. I wondered if the old path into town following the river was still there.

As it was getting late, Tristan showed me to the apartment door and left immediately as he had plans for dinner with Ben and his parents.

I took a deep breath as I let go of the handle of my suitcase to open the door to the studio apartment.

I'd lucked out in more ways than one, because not only did I have a place to stay for the week, but the apartment was also a picture postcard of country chic and looked very cozy.

It wasn't huge since it was a single room studio,

but it had a nice bed and two windows that faced the back of the building. There was an interconnecting door to the next apartment, so I hoped my neighbor, who Tristan said had also needed a place to stay at the last minute, wasn't too noisy, or I'd be able to hear everything through the thin door.

The first thing I needed to do was put my cell-phone on charge. I dreaded to think what kinds of emails I'd missed. I looked for my suitcase and noticed it was still in the hallway and the apartment door was open. God, I really needed a good night's sleep.

Everything happened too quickly. One moment I was reaching out for the suitcase, the next, something pulled my arm, and I found myself being dragged down.

I closed my eyes, bracing myself for impact. I let out a curse when my forearm dragged against some-thing sharp and then opened my eyes again when the landing was softer than I expected.

Dark brown eyes, so dark they were almost black, stared back at me. Warmth and a sense of rightness flooded my chest as I took in the face of the stranger, his defined jaw, perfect nose, five o'clock shadow, and those *eyes*.

I scrambled up, trying to get away from the man,

but ended up kneeing him in the groin. The poor guy let out a harsh groan and folded in on himself on the floor.

"Oh shit, crap, oh god. I'm so sorry." *For the love of god, Charlie.* I was horrified. The guy squirmed on the floor for a few minutes, taking deep breaths, before he was able to get up.

"Do you go around kicking everybody in the balls?" He coughed.

"No, only guys who tackle me to the floor," I answered without missing a beat.

The guy laughed. "You could have bought me dinner first."

My tummy rumbled at the mention of dinner, and the guy laughed again.

"You keep laughing at me, and I'll show you my other karate kicks," I teased.

"Sounds like you need dinner."

"Sounds like you're offering to buy." I didn't know what was wrong with me. Two seconds ago, I'd kicked the guy, and now, I was flirting unabashedly. I was never that forthcoming. Ever.

"What's your name?" he asked.

"Charlie, yours?"

"Kris."

I extended my hand to shake Kris's, and that's

when I saw a trickle of blood. "Crap, I haven't got any Band-Aids. Do you think there's a first aid kit anywhere in the apartment?"

"Come with me," Kris said.

I pulled the toppled suitcase into my apartment and then followed Kris to the apartment next door.

Kris opened his suitcase and rummaged for something.

"Got it," he said, pulling out a leather-bound box.

"What's that?" I asked.

"My first aid kit."

"You just happen to have a first aid kit."

"Yup."

"Why?"

"Sometimes I need it," Kris said.

"For you?"

"For other people."

I sat on the armchair by the window and Kris knelt beside me, taking an antiseptic wipe from the pack to clean my arm.

"Are you a doctor?" I asked.

Kris stopped for a second before continuing to clean the small cut. "Um…no, I train little soccer league, so I always have a kit with me."

A minute later, I was the proud carrier of a *Finding Nemo* Band Aid on my arm.

"My hero." I pretended to swoon. "I guess now I do owe you dinner."

"Technically, you fell because I pulled you down."

"Technically, you tripped on my suitcase."

We both smiled and time stopped as I once again fell momentarily under the spell of Kris's dark eyes. Never in my life had I felt the desire to get to know someone more than I did Kris. It was a strange feeling.

"How about we buy each other dinner?" I suggested.

"Deal."

"Then we better go find a place to eat before everyone is closed."

I was surprised to see Benny's Diner was still open. It had always been a popular diner, but after the mill closed, I thought it would have lost most of its customers.

There were a few other couples sitting on bar stools, so Kris picked a table that was placed under an arch, slightly hidden from view. Butterflies teased my stomach, and I felt a blush rise under my cheeks, so I opened the menu, hoping to hide my face.

"Hey, guys, what can I getcha?" the waitress said, more as a statement than a question.

"What would you recommend?" Kris asked.

"All the burgers are good, and I hear the hot dogs with the special fries are the best," she said.

"What's your favorite?" I asked.

"I'm vegetarian. Tell you what, leave it with me." The waitress scribbled something in her notepad and left.

"What just happened?" I asked.

"No clue, but I hope she knows what she's doing because there isn't a single vegetarian meal on this menu," Kris said with a laugh.

A minute later, the waitress appeared again with two milkshakes.

"By the way, guys, my name is Stephanie. Let me know if there's anything else I can get you."

We both stared at her as she walked away.

"Well, it sure looks like it's going to be anything but boring dining here," Kris said.

"I know, right? So, what brings you to Chester Falls?"

I hadn't missed the big suitcase in Kris's room and wondered how long he'd be staying.

"Oh, um, just some rest and recuperation. How about you?"

I told him about my sister's wedding and the lack of rooms at any hotels.

"If you're family, how come there wasn't a room for you?" Kris asked.

"Long story. I was meant to be in my childhood bedroom, but when I got home this afternoon, someone was already staying there."

"You didn't want to share a room with that guest?"

"It was a trap, so no, I didn't want to share. It's better for me to stay away from him."

Kris, fortunately, didn't ask any further questions, so we moved to other topics of conversation.

I couldn't remember the last time I'd had a real conversation with another guy just because we enjoyed each other's company. Well, I had Tom, but I'd known Tom for years, so that didn't count.

When we went back to our apartments, I sat on my bed and thought about the perplexing day I'd had. My hands itched to draw, so I reached out for my sketchpad and pencil box.

Picking a blank page, I started drawing the lines of Kris's face, the sexy five o'clock shadow, the perfect curve of his nose, and the deep richness of his eyes.

I really hoped tonight wasn't the last I'd see of Kris.

## 5

## KRIS

I'D NEVER BEEN a good sleeper when I was away from home. The fear of being recognized or my room being broken into always won out over whichever lavish surroundings I found myself in, and I just couldn't relax enough. Not having James around had added an extra element of unease, but oddly, I hadn't felt unsafe in Chester Falls.

Which was why I found it strange that I'd fallen asleep as soon as my head had hit the pillow last night, and I'd woken up feeling rested and energized.

I thought of Charlie sleeping in the apartment next door and wondered if he might have something to do with how I was feeling this morning. Who would've thought that having my man parts crushed by a knee would lead to such an interesting evening?

I stretched in the large, cozy bed and checked my cellphone for any messages from James. The phone was struggling to pick up signal. Normally I didn't have issues accessing mobile networks when I was abroad, so I could only put it down to the location of the building out of town. I'd need to go into town after breakfast to find a spot with better signal so I could check in with James.

My stomach growled, so I jumped off the bed and went to the bathroom to grab a shower, thinking of which casual clothes I'd be able to wear today. The thought put a spring in my step. Before the trip, I'd asked my secretary to source a suitable wardrobe, and he'd done a great job.

For the time I was in Chester Falls, and even when I returned to James's house, I wouldn't need to be Prince Kristof. I'd just be Kris. I'd wear jeans, cargo pants, and even shorts if the weather was agreeable enough.

When I stepped outside my room, I thought I heard some noise coming from Charlie's apartment. I stopped to listen if he was awake or maybe getting ready for breakfast too.

Last night, Charlie had looked like he'd enjoyed my company, even if sometimes he was a little quiet like he'd lost himself in his thoughts. I'd noticed that this normally came with a little blush that made the skin all around Charlie's neck a pretty pink shade and complimented his bright green eyes and red hair perfectly.

There was no question. Charlie was a very attractive man, and I was very attracted to him. He'd also mentioned an ex-boyfriend, so he was clearly gay, or at least bi. Not that it made any difference because I wasn't in Chester Falls to find love.

*What? Why was I thinking about love?* Thinking about the possibility of taking Charlie to bed was one thing, but love?

I was barely out of a long-term relationship; besides, nothing was going to happen anyway. At best I'd made a new friend I could be myself with. Charlie hadn't given any indication that he'd recognized me, even teasing me about picking the pickle out from the burger the waitress had chosen for me. The only people that had ever teased me in the same way were Aleks, Sergei, and James.

I shook my head and took a step in the direction of the stairs, feeling like a creep for the time I'd spent in the corridor outside the apartment. I'd barely moved before Charlie's room door opened and Charlie himself crashed into me.

My arms went instinctively around Charlie to

prevent him from getting hurt again. This time, we both managed to stay upright. I was glad our height difference meant Charlie's forehead had hit me on the chin, because had he been a few inches taller, we'd both be sporting bloody noses.

"I'm so sorry," Charlie said, looking at me with those eyes that reminded me of the clear water in the lake at the palace.

"You really must stop bumping into me like this," I said, struggling to keep a straight face.

"In my defense, there was no suitcase this time."

"In your defense, I was lurking."

Charlie's eyes went impossibly wide.

"You were?"

"I was trying to find the courage to knock on your door to see if you wanted to join me for breakfast and hoping to not come across as a total stalker." I surprised myself at how forward I was and also how good Charlie felt in my arms.

"You do know lurking outside someone's apartment can be considered stalkerish behavior, right?"

I grinned. "I was hoping you'd skirt past that little bit of detail."

We both smiled, and I didn't miss how soft and plush Charlie's lips looked.

"Why were you running out of your apartment, anyway?"

"Hungry."

"So…say I was to ask you to join me for breakfast. You'd say yes?"

"Dinner and breakfast?" Charlie shook his head. "This relationship is going too fast for me."

"Are you saying the wedding is off?"

Charlie laughed but then seemed to notice he was still in my arms and took a step back. I released him, albeit reluctantly, and noticed how Charlie blushed again. I wondered if kissing and sucking on Charlie's pale skin would leave a mark.

I coughed to get my thoughts into safe territory and took a step back to let Charlie lead the way.

"Do you think that diner from yesterday serves breakfast?" I asked.

Charlie looked at me with the widest grin.

"I take it they do," I said.

"They make the best pancakes in the world. Coffee is good too."

"You said the magic words. I will follow you forever," I said, pretending to faint.

Charlie blushed before he turned around to lead us out of the building. There were a few workmen around, but no one paid much attention to us as we stepped outside into the bright morning.

"Can we sit by the window?" Charlie asked when we arrived at Benny's Diner. "I didn't get to appreciate the view yesterday."

"Of course." I picked the table that gave us the best view of the grassy area that divided the diner and the Old Mill.

It was a sunny morning, and it didn't feel too cold. Would Charlie join me for a walk? He'd mentioned his sister's wedding last night, so maybe he had things to do.

My mood sank a little at the thought of Charlie being too busy to hang out with me. He was sweet and a great person to be around, not to mention the ease with which we flirted back and forth. Maybe it was selfish, but I wanted more.

"Good morning," the waiter, this time a guy, said as he filled two cups with coffee. "What can I get you for breakfast?"

"What's your favorite?" I asked.

The guy looked at me like I'd grown a second head.

"Ah, you're not from around here," he said, seemingly satisfied he'd found a reason for my question. "Momma Ruth's pancakes are the best. If you have a sweet tooth, I'd go for the cinnamon and applesauce, but the bacon and maple syrup are also good."

Charlie was biting his lip adorably while he looked at the menu as though he wanted to pick everything but knew he couldn't possibly eat it all.

"Can I get them both? They sound delicious, and I can't make up my mind."

Charlie looked up, wide-eyed, but then he smiled and ordered the ham, cheese, and mushroom omelet with a side of chocolate chip pancakes.

"I'm pretty sure we've ordered far more than we can eat," Charlie said.

"What can I say? I like trying new things," I said as I took a sip of the dark bitter coffee and hummed my appreciation.

Charlie laughed

"What? A guy needs his coffee," I said, "unless my country's spiced apple tea is available. I can never have enough of it, especially if it's iced."

*Shit.* I needed to pay better attention to what I said. Because Charlie was so easy to talk to, I was struggling to stop myself from running my mouth.

"Oh, where are you from?" Charlie asked.

"I…um…I'm from Lydovia."

"You're from Lydovia? That's awesome."

"Um, yes. I went to college in Boston, but I live there now."

"That must be why you don't have an accent. I love traveling, but I've never been to Lydovia," Charlie said.

"You must visit one day."

Charlie smiled that easy smile I was starting to like a lot.

"Would you like to go for a walk after breakfast?" I asked. "You don't have to if you're busy with wedding stuff."

"I'd love to," he said all too quickly. It gave me a warm feeling that he seemed to want to spend more time with me too.

The waiter turned up with our food. I didn't think either of us would be surprised if we couldn't finish it all because there was just too much of it. I'd forgotten how much bigger food portions were in America compared to Europe.

"This is delicious. I can't believe in all the years I lived in America I never tried it," I said as I finished half of the bacon and maple pancakes. The sweet and salty flavors were strange to my palate, but after a few bites, I understood why Americans loved the combination.

"They still make the best pancakes in the world,"

Charlie said. He took a piece of his pancake into his mouth and let out an appreciative moan. I stopped my coffee midway to my mouth and nearly spilled it all over my T-shirt.

"You okay?" Charlie asked.

"Oh yeah…yes, just being clumsy."

I adjusted myself in my seat to hide my body's reaction as a man wearing a yellow Benny's T-shirt approached our table.

"Good morning, Charlie, long time no see. Good morning…"

"Kris, just call me Kris."

"Kris, this is Benny, the old man who tries to pretend he owns the diner," Charlie joked but got up to give the man a hug.

"He's right too. Momma Ruth is the boss 'round here." He smiled even wider. "How were your pancakes? Been telling Momma to retire for months, so she's training someone new. Bless the kid, don't know how he hasn't quit yet."

"Must be her sunny disposition," Charlie said, and Benny let out one of those belly laughs that come from so deep inside you can't help feeling happy too.

"Well, if you need anything, please let me know. This one's on the house, alright boys? Make sure you come back tomorrow." And with an odd, knowing smile, he left.

"Hannah and I used to come here as kids. I didn't realize you had to pay for pancakes." Charlie chuckled to himself. "Sometimes Momma Ruth would call my parents and ask permission to feed us, but sometimes she'd make us a special pancake for free."

"Phone call. Shit," I blurted out as my phone buzzed in my pocket, causing me to jump. "I need to get in touch with my friend. He's waiting for my call, but I couldn't get a signal yesterday." Charlie narrowed his eyes but fortunately didn't call me out on my abrupt reaction.

"I'm sorry. I just need to check something. Can I meet you here in five for our walk?"

"Sure."

My cellphone had signal, albeit weak, but it seemed to work when I dialed James's number. It rang a few times before he answered.

"Kris, Jesus man, I was about to SWAT team you."

"Sorry, I had no signal yesterday. Everything's okay, so there's no need to worry. I've been to a local diner, but no one recognized me, just as you'd said."

"Benny's? Damn, I miss their pancakes."

James updated me on the press situation, which hadn't changed, so it looked like I'd be staying in Chester Falls for now.

I ended the call and saw Benny clearing some tables.

"Mr... Benny," I called.

"Oh, Kris, can I help with anything? Are you looking for suggestions on activities you can do with your Charlie?" That last part was said in a whisper as he leaned closer and gave me a knowing smile.

If I'd had a lighter complexion, I knew for sure my blush would have been very visible at Benny's insinuation that Charlie may be more than a friend.

Benny pointed me to a display stand full of leaflets for activities available in Chester Falls and the surrounding area. I picked a few that looked interesting. I hoped I could do some with Charlie, but I tried to manage my own expectations on that front.

On my way back to meet Charlie, I picked up a flask full of freshly brewed coffee from Benny. He even gave me a small bag with a few of Momma Ruth's cookies inside. He said they were Charlie's favorite.

My heart fell when I walked back to the table and Charlie wasn't there.

# 6

## CHARLIE

As SOON AS I stepped outside through the double doors of the diner, I took a deep breath. I let it out and then took another one. I loved the smell of the country in the morning when it was still so fresh and clean with morning dew.

When I was young, my family used to laugh when I'd said mornings like these smelled like green. Of course, you couldn't smell color, but it was the scent of freshly cut grass that was still wet, and you could only really smell it properly when you were in the country surrounded by trees and flowers and other green things. So yes, for me this would always be the smell of green.

It was a mild morning, so I knew that unless the

weather changed dramatically, which was unlikely, it would be a great day to explore.

I felt the urge to draw what I saw: the green grass that took up most of the square with patches of wildflowers contrasting with the imposing industrial building of the Old Mill. It was a shame my sketchbook was in the apartment.

I noticed a man on his knees next to a number of small plant pots in one corner of the grassy square. He looked too tall to be in that position comfortably. The way the sun hit him made his light brown hair look like copper, and the brightness of his white long-sleeved cotton shirt created a bright halo around him. He also wore navy cargo pants with more pockets than was fashionably advisable in my opinion, but I guessed the man's choice of clothing was more practical than anything. The man was also barefoot.

Curiosity won me over. I looked into the diner, but Kris wasn't back, so I walked over to the man.

"Good morning," I said.

"Oh, good morning, my friend. It is a fine morning, isn't it? Perfect for repotting these little seedlings."

"I did wonder what you were doing. My grandmother loved gardening. I used to help her in her yard when I was a kid."

The man stretched his arm out to me. "I'm Oleander, but most people call me Olly. I'm the town gardener. Would you like to give your rusty green fingers a new memory?"

"Oh, I'd love to, but I'm waiting for my friend. I'm Charlie, by the way."

"What brings you to Chester Falls, Charlie?"

"My sister is getting married this weekend."

"That is a happy occasion. Congratulations."

"Thank you. Did you plant all the wildflowers?" I asked, looking at the various patches that complemented perfectly the manicured lawn.

"Oh yes, it takes a lot of skill. To get that effect you need to make sure the seeds for each kind of flower are spread evenly."

"Really?"

Olly slapped his knees and laughed. "Nah, I'm just teasing."

I smiled, remembering the old town gardener, Basil. Olly was every bit as eccentric.

"Your friend is looking for you."

I turned toward the diner, and true enough, Kris was standing by our table looking around. I waved to get his attention, but Kris didn't seem to see me. I waved again and luckily this time Kris saw me.

His smile took my breath away. We walked to

each other and stopped when we were only inches apart outside the diner.

"Thought you'd ditched me," Kris said with a tentative smile.

"I would never do that. I mean, who would I keep bumping into?"

Kris's smile most definitely reached his eyes now. And man, did they light up. It made the butterflies in my stomach flutter.

"I was chatting to Olly; he's repotting some seedlings."

I pointed at the gardener and excused myself to pick up my smaller sketchbook and box of pencils from the apartment.

On my return, I found Kris crouched next to Olly, chatting away. As I approached, I overheard Olly saying, "Plant the seeds together, your love will grow forever."

I couldn't see Kris's face as he took in the small bag of seeds Olly placed in his hand. Olly looked up and smiled at me. Kris turned around so quickly he lost balance and ended up sitting on the grass.

"Nothing to do with me this time," I said, holding my hands up before I held one out to help Kris.

"Thanks," Kris said after dusting off some dirt from his jeans. "Shall we go explore, then?"

Kris put the bag with the seeds in his pocket and picked up a flask and another bag he'd placed on a nearby seat.

"We have coffee and cookies, thanks to Benny," Kris said, holding the goodies up.

"He's always been my favorite person." I grinned.

We started off in the direction of the Old Mill, turning right onto a path that followed the river's contour into town.

Olly's words were playing on my mind. *Plant the seeds together, your love will grow forever.* Was he referring to a boyfriend or girlfriend Kris had back in Lydovia? For some reason, the thought made my stomach sink.

When I'd overheard Olly, part of me thought that maybe Olly had made an assumption and was referring to Kris and me, which was ridiculous. After all, we'd only just met, we were in Chester Falls temporarily, and I wasn't even sure Kris was gay.

Kris carried himself with such grace as though he was on a catwalk. I thought about the expensive suits I sold at work and the designer labels. It was clear from Kris's outfit that he had a lot of money. His casual clothes would have cost me more than a month's wages, and I was pretty sure the shirt Kris had on wasn't even on sale in department stores.

It didn't matter anyway.

"What doesn't matter?" Kris asked.

"What?"

"You said, 'it doesn't matter, anyway.'"

"Oh, er, nothing important. I was thinking about, er, nothing. Why are you here?" I blurted out as an attempt to change the subject.

"Just rest—"

"And recuperation, yes, you said last night. You're wearing designer clothes, and you're from one of the richest countries in Europe. You could be anywhere: a spa hotel, a Scottish castle. Why here?"

Kris looked down, and I felt bad for asking. I didn't want to pry, but I was curious.

"It's complicated."

"I'm a good listener," I said.

We came to a set of stone steps that led right into the water. It was the perfect place.

"Let's sit here. Why don't you buy me coffee and a cookie?" I winked.

Kris smiled, looking a little more relaxed as he sat next to me and unscrewed the cups from the top of the flask so he could pour the hot coffee.

I took my sketchbook and pencils from my small

rucksack and opened it on a blank page. Kris narrowed his eyes, so I clarified.

"I like drawing. Now, you talk. Charlie listen," I said as I picked the right pencil for what I had in mind.

Kris sighed. "Okay. My ex did something that made it look like I'd done it. The press jumped on it, so now I'm here hiding until I have to attend an event in a few weeks."

I looked up. "Are you like, a famous person, or something?"

"Or something."

Kris leaned forward, resting his elbows on his knees and holding the coffee cup in his hands.

We were silent for a moment. I noticed the strong lines of Kris's fingers, the small veins I could see under the skin, and the perfect nails. Kris caressed the rim of the cup with his thumb, and I wondered what it would be like to feel Kris's touch. Would it be soft and light? Or would it be strong and rough? I wasn't sure I minded which, as long as it came from Kris.

I barely even noticed what I was drawing anymore. It was like the pencil had a mind of its own. When Kris gripped the cup harder, the pencil pressed harder on the paper, creating darker lines.

"I knew we wouldn't be together forever," Kris

said, "but he was, is, my best friend. He's the only one I could ever tell everything. I'm afraid I may have messed that up too."

"If he was your best friend, surely you can work it out."

Kris took a sip of the coffee, put the cup down, and took a cookie out of the bag. It was a chocolate cookie with chocolate chips, my favorite. Normally, I would have squealed and taken my own cookie out of the bag, but I couldn't take my eyes off Kris now.

All around us was nature, the river, trees, wild-flowers, and the occasional duck or swan would swim past us. I was aware of it all, but my eyes were locked on Kris's mouth as he took a bite of the cookie, chewed it, and then swallowed. His Adam's apple bobbing up and down with the movement.

I wanted to take it all in so I could draw it later on my bigger pad. My eyes were like magnifying glasses, zeroing in on the uneven hairs of Kris's short stubble, his eyes that looked so dark they were almost black, and the little beauty mark right under Kris's earlobe that looked like a crescent moon.

Kris looked at me and our gazes locked. I'd never in my life wanted to kiss someone more. Not even when I'd been in the secret relationship with Rory did I ever feel the same way. Sure, I'd enjoyed kissing

Rory, but after we broke up, I'd always wondered if I'd just enjoyed the excitement of trying not to get caught.

"Charlie." Kris's deep and raspy voice brought me out of my head, and I sat up just a little straighter.

"I'm sorry, I was just…er, you have great lines."

"I have *what*?" Kris chuckled.

I covered my face with my hands to hide my embarrassment. I'd never minded my red hair and pasty white skin much, they were just part of who I was, but as I'd grown older, I'd realized how my outside was just a mirror image of the inside, as though I was totally transparent.

From between my fingers, I saw Kris pick up the small sketchbook from where it had fallen by my feet.

"Charlie."

I looked up. Kris was staring at the drawing.

"I'm sorry. It's not great. Maybe I should have drawn one of the swans. That would have been easier. It's just, er…the way you were holding the cup and your hands. I really wanted to draw them."

"This is beautiful. Honestly. I didn't know you were an artist."

"I'm not. I'm just a manager in the menswear department of a store. I sell expensive clothes to men with more money than fashion sense. That's all."

Kris put his hand on mine, and I looked at where they connected.

"See my hand?" he asked. "How it curves as I hold on to yours? It's organic, it's real, and it can move."

I closed my eyes as Kris's fingers caressed the skin of my knuckles. I took a deep breath and opened my eyes again.

"You drew my hand like it was a living thing. I know it sounds ridiculous, but I can see my feelings in that drawing, in the way my hand is gripping the mug. You have a rare talent, Charlie."

Kris's words hit me right in the place I'd kept closed off so I didn't have to face the reality that drawing was my life passion, and without it, I simply existed without living. Kris's words hit me right in the heart.

"Charlie, can I ask you something?"

"Sure," I choked.

"Will you draw me?"

# 7

## KRIS

I DIDN'T KNOW what possessed me to ask Charlie to draw my picture. I hadn't liked the lack of self-confidence that came out of Charlie when he'd looked at the drawing. It was such a simple but perfect sketch of my hands curled around the coffee cup. I saw life in it. I saw the frustration and sadness I'd felt when I'd told Charlie about messing my friendship up with Sergei.

Or maybe it was a lot simpler than that; I wanted any excuse to spend more time with Charlie. I wanted to get to know him beyond the superficial stuff we'd talked about last night over dinner.

Charlie was gentle and kind. Sergei would have chewed the head off Stephanie for assuming what he'd want for dinner, and he would have ordered something else just to spite her. He would have demanded the most expensive wine on the list instead of whatever local ale they had on draft. Not that Sergei was a bad person or a spoiled one; he'd simply grown up in a world where he'd had to build a certain amount of armor to fit in.

Charlie and Sergei couldn't be more different on the surface, and I wanted more of Charlie. To run my hands through Charlie's red hair, to touch the skin running down from his neck to his chest and see if it blushed under my touch too.

"What?" Charlie asked, his eyes like a deer in the headlights.

"Would you draw me?"

"Oh, er, I don't know. Are you sure?"

"Absolutely." I took another cookie out of the bag and gave it to Charlie. He licked his lips before he took a bite.

"These are my favorite cookies in the world," Charlie said, his mouth full.

"I'll have to thank Benny."

We drank the rest of the coffee and finished the cookies in the bag. Well, Charlie had most of them, which I had really enjoyed watching.

"Charlie, can I see more of your drawings?"

Charlie hesitated but then took the sketchbook from his rucksack and passed it to me.

The picture on the first page was of two pigeons side by side on a power line. Even though the drawing was in pencil, it was incredibly detailed with enough shades of gray that it made the birds look real. Each picture after that was exactly the same. It was as if Charlie could feel what the subject of his drawings was feeling, and when it was an inanimate subject, he gave them purpose, a place in the world.

"I don't know what to say, Charlie. This is beautiful. You said you work in a store. Why?" I asked.

"What do you mean?"

"Why aren't you an artist?"

He looked down and played with a small pebble that was near his shoe.

"I'll rephrase that. You are an artist, Charlie. Why isn't this your job?"

Charlie got up and started walking. I stumbled up, grabbing our belongings and catching up with Charlie.

"Wait, I'm sorry. I didn't mean to upset you."

"You're not upsetting me. I want to be an artist. It's all I ever wanted to be," Charlie said.

"Then why?"

"It's not easy to sell your art when you don't have

connections. When I finished my degree, I was one of many talented artists," Charlie said, raising his hands to quote the word talented. "Some had trust funds, parents with connections, or luck. I had none of those, and I couldn't go home, so I found a job in retail."

"Why couldn't you go home?"

Charlie walked in silence, kicking little stones here and there. I didn't want to press the subject, but I wanted to understand, and at the moment, I didn't.

I wasn't sure how long it would take to get to town, but I hoped by the time we got there I'd be able to make Charlie feel better. I thought of the leaflets I had in my pockets with the local activities.

"I didn't want to prove him right. That's why I didn't go home."

"Who?"

"Rory, my ex. He always said art was a pointless degree, that I would never make a decent living and would always struggle. He was right."

I had the sudden urge to punch this Rory guy. Who the hell did he think he was to tell Charlie he couldn't follow his dreams or do something he was clearly born to do?

Charlie stopped and faced me.

"It doesn't matter anyway," he said.

He looked sad and resigned.

I took a step closer to Charlie and put my hands on either side of his face, tilting Charlie's head up so I could see his beautiful green eyes.

"It matters, Charlie," I said, no louder than a whisper. "Your dreams matter. You matter."

A small tear escaped Charlie's eye, and I caught it with my thumb.

"I'm sorry, I didn't want to upset you."

Charlie rested his hands on my waist and shook his head. My heart skipped a beat at the easy way in which Charlie leaned on me.

"You didn't upset me. I guess this is a sore subject made worse because I'll have to face him at the wedding."

"Why is he going to be at the wedding if you're no longer together?"

"He's my brother's best friend, and he's been around so long he's like part of the family." Charlie sighed. "Our relationship was a secret."

"So, when you said yesterday staying at your parents was a trap…"

"He's having work done at his place, and since he's helping out with the wedding… I didn't know he was crashing in my room. He told everyone he'd be happy to share with me."

I had a renewed hatred for Rory now for using Charlie's sister's wedding as an opportunity to get to Charlie, and right under his family's nose.

The unexpected urge to pull Charlie even closer and wrap my arms around him was strong. I wanted to give Charlie something, but I wasn't sure what, so I offered comfort and empathy.

Charlie's head fitted so perfectly in the crook of my neck. I didn't even try to stop myself from breathing in the scent of Charlie's hair. It smelled of green apples, fresh and sweet.

"Thank you," Charlie said into my chest.

"Any time."

We parted and carried on our walk by the river. Charlie was still more silent than I'd have liked, but he didn't seem as upset.

"I've been looking forward to my sister's wedding for months. I didn't think he'd be here. His parents travel a lot, but once a year around this time, they all get together and go on vacation to Cape Cod. He must have canceled it to come to the wedding."

I couldn't do anything about the wedding and Rory, but maybe I could do something for Charlie.

"Do you trust me?"

Charlie looked at me from the corner of his eye with raised brows.

"Let me think. Since I've met you, I've been dragged down to the floor, injured my arm, crashed into you, and I've had strangers picking my meals. You're the common denominator here so..." He shrugged.

I laughed. "Okay, but since you met me, you've had personalized medical care, great company, and the best cookies in the world, so..." I shrugged as though it was enough to balance Charlie's argument.

"You have a point; those cookies were pretty great. And there was the hug too. I enjoyed that."

My belly was suddenly full of butterflies. The return of Charlie's easy smile did things to me I was only beginning to accept could happen with someone other than Sergei for the first time in my life.

"Argument settled. How would you feel about—"

"Charlie?"

I was interrupted by a woman calling Charlie's name from a distance.

Charlie picked up his pace to meet the woman, so I figured they knew each other. She was wearing the tightest workout outfit, and I wondered how she could even breathe without tearing the stitches out. Her face was also fully made up. An interesting contrast, I thought.

"Hi, Aunt G. What are you doing here?"

"Hi, darling," she said, kissing Charlie on both cheeks. "These champagne breakfasts are delightful, but they are not good for my waist. You know a girl of a certain age needs to make an extra effort." She got closer to Charlie as though she was going to tell him a secret. "Guess who's not coming to the wedding?"

"I don't really—"

"Gary and Lisa Rich. Apparently…" She looked around so no one would overhear, even though there was no one else around apart from Charlie and I. "Apparently, Gary was having an affair with the neighbors' daughter who's a teaching assistant at the college, and because all their money was Lisa's, she kicked him out of the house."

"Does this mess up Hannah's seating plan?"

It didn't surprise me that the first thing out of Charlie's mouth was worry for his sister.

"No, I don't think so. Speaking of the seating plan, Rory has been asking for you, something about helping him do something for Connor?"

"Oh."

"Anyway, I can tell him I saw you."

"Um, that's okay Aunt G."

Charlie's posture was so rigid I was afraid he'd snap in two.

"Good morning, Ma'am, how do you do?" I said, making eye contact and holding out my hand to Charlie's aunt. Her eyes bulged like she hadn't noticed I'd had been there all along.

"Oh, hi…hello."

I brought her hand up for a gentle kiss on her knuckles, and she let out a sigh. I smiled to myself; the old trick always worked.

She was still holding onto my hand when she asked Charlie, "Darling, who is this delightfully polite young man? Not to mention delectable."

Charlie took half a step closer to me as though he was prepared to defend me against his aunt's claws. I chuckled.

"Aunt G, this is Kris. Kris, this is my aunt, Gina. She's not normally a sex-crazed wildcat with sharp claws, but it must be mating season."

I laughed.

"Oh, shut up. I'm barely a house cat," she purred. "So, Kris, what are your intentions with my favorite nephew here?"

I felt heat rising up my face, and I wasn't sure even my tanned complexion could hide it when I was under the scrutiny of Charlie's Aunt Gina.

"Oh, I…" I looked at Charlie for help, but Charlie looked tongue-tied too.

"Oh, come on, boys. You don't have to hide from me. You must be the boyfriend Charlie's parents told me about. I know a couple in love when I see one."

She pointed one of her long, red, manicured nails into Charlie's chest. "I don't know why you had to hide your boyfriend away, Charlie. Your parents are going to be disappointed."

"No, Aunt—" Charlie tried to interrupt, but there was no stopping Gina.

"You listen to me. Your parents will be upset if they know you brought your boyfriend with you and haven't introduced him to them. Without Gary and Lisa at the wedding, there are two seats at my table, so you can sit with us instead of sitting on your own at the singles table."

If Charlie was going to be sitting at the singles table, he'd no doubt be right next to Rory. That thought didn't sit well with me.

"Thank you, Gina, I'd love to attend the wedding if that won't be too much of an inconvenience."

I pulled Charlie by the waist and placed a kiss on his cheek. "It'll be fun, won't it, sweetheart?"

Charlie looked at me with impossibly wide eyes and said under his breath, "What are you doing?"

"It won't be any trouble at all," Gina said. "I shall go tell the venue to update the seating plan right away. Buh-bye for now." She turned on her heel and left.

I smiled at her departing figure and then turned to Charlie who was looking back at me with murderous eyes.

# 8

## CHARLIE

"WHAT THE HELL JUST HAPPENED?" I asked.

Panic rose in my chest. Why didn't Kris say anything when Gina assumed he was my boyfriend? And why would he agree to come to the wedding as my plus one?

Kris's face fell. "Charlie, I…I'm sorry. I overstepped my mark."

"Why didn't you set her straight?"

"When Gina said you'd be at the singles table, I…I don't know. I thought you might not want to sit with Rory. Please forgive me?" Kris touched my cheek, which was still tingling from the too-brief kiss he'd planted there earlier. I tried to calm down, but my pulse increased from Kris's touch.

"In what world do you think anyone would

believe you and I are dating?" I said, my voice cracking slightly. I was annoyed with myself that I wasn't able to feel as strong and confident as Kris had looked when he'd lied to Gina.

"What do you mean?" Kris looked at me with confusion.

"What do you mean, what do I mean? Look at you, Kris." I took a step back, checking Kris from head to toe. "You walk with the confidence of a prince and you dress like one too. I'm just...I don't know. Would you ever have noticed me if you hadn't fallen over my suitcase?"

Kris flinched, and I took it as a sign I was right. I started walking toward town. I needed to catch up with Gina to stop her from opening her mouth.

Kris called out to me, but I kept walking until I felt my hand being pulled and was forced to turn around. In a heartbeat, I found myself in Kris's arms for the third time today.

"Charlie, I would have noticed you even if I hadn't seen you. It's near enough impossible to not be drawn to you, your kindness, the way you see the world, the way you draw the world. I would have always noticed you. Even if I was blind, I would have known you were there."

I stared at Kris, not knowing what to say. That was until my stupid mouth decided to speak for me.

"Are you even gay?" I put both my hands on my mouth to stop any more stupid words from coming out.

Kris chuckled and put his hands on mine to pull them down. Everything happened in slow motion; Kris traced the outline of my bottom lip, dragged his thumb down toward my chin, and then tilted my head up.

I couldn't believe what was happening even as our lips met, my heart beating at a thousand miles per second as Kris sucked gently on my lip. An audible sigh escaped me, which I normally would have been embarrassed about, except Kris's tongue touched mine, and suddenly I was in a whole new world where my brain was mush and my body was a firework display inside.

Kris's arms tightened around me, and I took the opportunity to run my fingers through Kris's hair. I never wanted this kiss to end. I never wanted this feeling to disappear.

The one long, sweet, sexy kiss gave way to smaller kisses until I regained my breathing and brain function back. I finally drew my lips from Kris's. "Okay… so, you're gay."

Kris's eyes were impossibly dark, and his lids were only half open. The corners of his mouth raised. "I am."

I breathed in, taking in the intoxicating smell of Kris's aftershave and wondering if it would be okay to lick his neck. I shook my head to rid it of the thought.

"But that doesn't mean you need to pretend to be my boyfriend just so I don't have to sit with Rory at the wedding."

"What if I wanted to?" Kris said.

"What?" Did Kris mean what I thought he meant? Did he really want to pretend to be my boyfriend? But we'd barely met and didn't know anything about each other.

"I'd like to help you, be your date for the wedding and your fake boyfriend."

"Oh." I tried my best to hide the little pang of disappointment that hit me. Kris was offering to be my buffer so I didn't have to deal with Rory. It was temporary. I thought about it. Maybe we could have some fun together, and then when it was all over, we'd each go our separate ways. Who knew, maybe we'd even remain friends.

"Why?" Charlie asked.

"I don't know. Because you're sweet and gorgeous, and I am a sucker for a lost cause."

I punched Kris's arm.

"Okay, fine. Let's do it."

Kris smiled and kissed me again. God, kissing Kris was perfection, and I never wanted to stop.

"I guess we need to get to know each other better," Kris said between kisses.

"Oh, yes please." Now that was an idea I was well behind.

"I meant really get to know each other, Charlie."

I was mortified. Of course, Kris meant the exchanging-of-information kind of getting to know each other, not the kind that had popped into my head that involved rumpled bedsheets and naked skin.

Kris gave me another long, deep kiss. How was I meant to get the right idea when Kris kept giving me the wrong one?

When we came up for air, Kris whispered into my mouth, "I do want to get to know you that way." Which was evident from the bulge I felt against my own. "But if the rest of your family are anything like Gina, I'm going to need some preparation."

"Shall I write down some notes, like their names and stuff?" I asked.

"Nope, I have a better idea."

"What's that?"

Kris took a leaflet out of his pocket and unfolded it before handing it to me.

"We're going indoor climbing." Kris grinned as he took my hand, interlacing our fingers, and started to walk back toward the Old Mill.

It took a few seconds for my brain to catch up with what I'd heard because I'd been staring at our joined hands, taking a mental picture to draw later.

"No, no, no, no, NO!" I squeaked. "Do you want to kill me?" When the hell did Chester Falls get indoor climbing facilities anyway? There certainly hadn't been any when I'd lived here.

"Not at all. I want you to chill and think about something else other than the wedding or Rory. Climbing is the perfect activity."

I wasn't so sure. I wasn't exactly afraid of heights, but the thought of hanging on a wall attached to a piece of string—okay, rope—got my hands damp and gave me the wrong kind of butterflies.

---

My heart rate was fighting a losing battle as Kris helped me into the harness.

"I'm sure I should be enjoying having you strap me in more than I am, but I'm too terrified."

Kris laughed, but when our eyes met, I realized Kris's thoughts weren't too far from my own.

Before going to the local gym where the climbing walls were, we'd stopped by Kris's apartment to get his gear, and so we could both grab more appropriate clothing. I was surprised to know Kris had his own stuff, but then he went on to explain that he loved climbing and always took his kit with him on the off-chance he had an opportunity to enjoy one of his favorite hobbies.

My harness and shoes were hired from the gym after Kris assured me they were perfectly safe and in good condition. Kris's experience climbing was reassuring, but it still didn't stop me from feeling nervous. The wall was so high, and I couldn't see how on earth I'd be able to hold on to the tiny colorful hand grabby things, whatever they were called.

Kris put his harness on and went over to speak to a guy who wore a gym branded T-shirt, so I figured he worked here.

I placed my hand on the wall and ran it over the surface, feeling the rough texture under my fingers, gripping one of the holds to test it. It wasn't very big.

How would I be able to hold onto it when gravity was doing her best to bring me down?

"Charlie?"

I jumped when I heard Kris call. Jeez, I needed to calm down.

"This is Brad. He works here, so he's going to belay for me so you can see how I do it, okay?"

"He's going to do what?"

"Belay. That means he's going to stay on the ground and keep my rope tight for me so I'm safe if I fall."

I looked at Brad. He was a few inches shorter than me and a whole lot lighter. How was he going to be able to hold Kris up there? I looked at Kris, then at Brad, and then Kris again.

"No, he can't do it," I said.

Kris looked confused.

"He's too small! How is he going to hold you if you fall? He'll go up as you go down, and then you'll—"

Kris put his hands on my shoulders. "Let me explain how it works. You see this little device here?" He pointed at a metal thing that was attached to Brad's harness by a carabiner.

"Yes, what's that?"

"This is the belay," Brad said. "Let me show you how it works."

Brad made a very complicated knot with the rope that was attached to a metal bar at the top of the wall. He tried to talk me through it, but I lost track after the second loop around the figure of eight. Kris's rope did look very secure, but I still wasn't convinced that if he fell from the wall Brad wouldn't go flying up.

"Charlie, Kris is going up now. See how the rope is tight? Every time he goes up and the rope slacks, I pull this end, keep it tight, and then lock it that way so, if he does slip, he will only come down by a few feet."

"Okay, if you say so," I said, still in doubt, and then said to Kris, "Please don't fall."

"I will try my best not to." Kris winked, and my belly butterflies fluttered.

Once Kris added some chalk to his hands, he was ready to climb.

I couldn't take my eyes off Kris as he climbed the wall effortlessly. Each time he picked a hold for his hands or feet, Brad explained why Kris had chosen that particular route.

Apparently, if you wanted to make things hard for yourself, you had to pick holds of a particular color.

"Are you okay?" I shouted at Kris who'd stopped when he was halfway up.

"He's okay. He's thinking. Sometimes you have to stop when you're in a comfortable place so you can have a look at the route above and decide where you want to go," Brad explained.

Kris looked down, releasing one of his hands to wave. I gasped. Kris did a little wiggle and shouted back, "Does my butt look big in this?"

"Looks fucking perfect," I muttered to myself as I shook my head at Kris for being so calm as to make jokes while hanging from a rope attached to the skinniest guy I'd ever seen working for a gym.

"Doesn't it just," Brad agreed, and my head snapped to look at Brad who was admiring Kris's butt as he resumed the climb, reaching the top in a few easy moves.

"What did you say?"

"Oh, um, I'm sorry, I didn't mean…crap." Brad looked embarrassed to have been caught admiring Kris. "I'm sorry, I didn't realize you were together. And it was very inappropriate of me to comment."

I looked down at the floor. "We're not together. Well, we are, kinda. It's complicated." I sighed.

"Can I come down?" Kris called from the top of the wall.

Brad coughed and carried on explaining that Kris was going to abseil down while he controlled the descent using the belay.

It wasn't until Kris had both his feet back on the ground that I was able to relax. I couldn't help myself from going over to Kris and putting my arms around him.

Kris's laugh was a sign he'd made it back down safe and that made me smile too. That was, until, he said, "It's your turn now."

# 9

## KRIS

CHARLIE'S FACE was beyond adorable when he pouted, but I wanted to behave in a public place, so no matter how soft and kissable Charlie's lips looked, I was going to be good.

The climb had been pretty easy, so I'd pushed myself by picking the hardest route. It still wasn't the highest-grade wall I'd climbed, and it was no match for outdoor climbing, but since I hadn't had any warm-up, the wall had been a suitable challenge. I'd also noticed a number of easier routes with good foot and handholds for Charlie, so I'd mapped those in my mind so I could guide him.

When I'd come back down, Brad had excused himself and went over to the other side of the hall to tidy some equipment. I wondered if anything had happened between Charlie and Brad, but since Charlie was happily in my arms, I didn't really care about anything else.

"Do I have to climb?" Charlie asked, looking up from my chest.

"You don't, but I guarantee if you try, you're going to love it. You don't have to go all the way up, so just have a go and see how you feel, okay?"

Charlie nodded. I could tell that he was reluctant for obvious reasons, but he was also curious.

I tied the rope to Charlie's harness and then set up his side of the rope through the belay, pulling it tighter than necessary to show him there wouldn't be any slack.

"Are you ready?"

"No."

I chuckled.

"Forget about the colors, go for the hold that feels more comfortable. Don't rush up, take your time to think about where you want to go next. And the biggest rule of all. You need to push with your legs, not pull with your arms. It'll be a lot easier if you use your legs more."

"Okay."

I placed a soft kiss on Charlie's lips. "I won't let you fall."

"You better keep that promise, or else."

There was nothing I wouldn't do to keep my promise to Charlie as I made sure the rope was always tighter than usual to make him feel safe.

Charlie's first moves were slow and tentative. He'd come down a couple of times when he wasn't sure how to keep going, so I'd talked him through it until he remembered where to put his hands and feet so he wasn't getting himself stuck in a position.

I could hear Charlie muttering to himself as he was moving on the wall but couldn't understand a word. He was just too adorable and cute, and I was rapidly forgetting why it was a bad idea to get involved with someone. Even if it was only a pretend and temporary relationship, and even if it was to keep Charlie away from his ex's sneaky advances. As it was, I already liked Charlie more than I should.

"Kris, I'm stuck," Charlie called.

He wasn't, but I understood how from Charlie's point of view it would seem that there was no way for him to go in one smooth move.

"Charlie, I'm tightening your rope. Sit back on the harness."

"Are you insane?"

I chuckled. "It's okay, I've got you. Sit back. Do it slowly if you're afraid."

Charlie's legs shook as he pushed away from the wall very slowly and allowed the harness and the rope to take his weight.

"Good, you're doing well. Do you see where you had your left hand?"

"Yes?"

"That's going to be a foothold."

"Not gonna happen."

"It will, you just need to take smaller steps. Look at the wall and see if you can figure out where you need to put your hands and your feet. Remember, you're pushing yourself up with your legs so you can use the smaller holds for your hands."

I let Charlie work out for himself how to continue the climb. When I was up on the wall, everything else ceased to exist. The burn in my muscles told me to be efficient, smart, and to keep going because the feeling you got when your feet were back on the ground was the most amazing thing, and I wanted Charlie to experience that.

After a minute or so, Charlie continued his climb. He'd taken my advice to take smaller steps, which helped get his feet on the right holds. I couldn't see Charlie's face, but everything about him showed concentration, focus, and determination.

When Charlie reached the top, he held onto the top metal bar over the wall as though he was holding on for his life, but when he looked down toward me, he was beaming.

"I did it! Oh my god, Kris, I did it."

There was no more space in my heart at that moment because it was full of pride for Charlie. I'd known he could do it, but seeing him struggle and never give up told me everything I needed to know about Charlie. More than a list of relatives' names or what his favorite food was.

"You were amazing. Well done. Ready to come down?" I asked.

"Okay, what do I do?"

"Do what you did earlier. Sit down on the harness. I will lower you down now."

Charlie sat back, but he was reluctant to let go of the wall, so I lowered him slowly, allowing Charlie to keep hold of the wall as he was descending.

As soon as Charlie's feet were on the floor he threw himself at me, wrapping his legs around my waist and claiming my mouth. I took a few steps back from the surprise of having Charlie jump me but regained my footing and then walked forward until I had Charlie pressed against the wall.

It was a mystery as to how I hadn't tripped over the ropes on the floor, but I didn't care because I had Charlie wrapped around me like he was just where he belonged. Our tongues dueled for dominance, and the sweet, sometimes shy Charlie had been replaced by someone who wasn't afraid to go for what he wanted. He didn't even seem to mind that he probably had the holds on the wall digging against his back.

"Christ, Charlie, are you trying to kill me?" I said, struggling to draw a breath, my heart rate increased, not to mention the bulge in my shorts.

"Life, death situation."

"Alive, you are very alive," I said, pressing Charlie farther into the wall and taking another kiss.

A cough from the other side of the room reminded me that we weren't alone, so I placed Charlie back on the floor with some reluctance.

Charlie looked over my shoulder and straightened his T-shirt and his shorts. "Shall we go take a shower and then grab something to eat? I'm ravenous."

I agreed. I could definitely do with a cold shower after having Charlie's slim body pressed against mine, although now I wasn't so sure if it was a good idea to be in the proximity of a naked Charlie.

In the end, we did keep our hands off each other, thanks to the individual shower cubicles during the shortest and most frustrating shower in history, but I didn't miss Charlie's sudden shyness. If only Charlie had seen what his presence was doing to me.

I'd never thought about Lydovia's internal politics or replayed old soccer tactics in my head so much before as I did in those ten minutes, which also reminded me I needed to call Aleks for an update on the press situation.

Not that I was eager to go home now. Meeting Charlie had certainly made the short exile a lot more interesting, even if I had to be careful about getting too involved. After all, even though we were both single and free to pursue a relationship, I was a prince with a reputation, and Charlie was just too good for someone like me.

I didn't speak to Charlie until we were both fully dressed and walking back to the Old Mill. It was less tempting that way.

"When do you have to see your family?"

Charlie went from relaxed to super tense in the blink of an eye.

"Are you okay?" I asked.

"Yes, I guess. Just nervous about this whole fake boyfriend thing."

"Hey, don't worry," I said. "There won't be a single person at the wedding who will doubt that we are madly in love."

Charlie looked like he wasn't so sure.

"Are you doubting my acting skills?" I teased, bumping my shoulder against Charlie's.

Charlie kept his eyes on the ground. I wanted to know what was bothering him so I could fix it.

"No, it's...never mind, you're right. It'll be fine."

I knew my family was different from most royal families. Aleks and I hadn't even known our parents were royalty and that we were a royal prince and princess until we were old enough to understand it.

I'd only really grasped the reality when my mom had died and suddenly every news headline was about the young prince and princess that had lost their mom so young. As we'd grown up, every move we'd made was reported as though it was a direct cause of losing a parent.

It hit me then. Charlie didn't want to deceive his family. It was one thing giving Rory the wrong impression, but another to do it to his family.

"Mom and Dad are the best," Charlie said. "Hannah has always had her own individual style, colored hair that changed every week, clothes she made herself, and she was a bright, bubbly girly girl. When she told them she wanted to be a lawyer and specialize in family law, the only thing they said was for her to never lose her individuality no matter where she worked, because the families she'd be working for were just like her. Real."

I took Charlie's hand in mine as we walked. I saw a blush and small smile tease Charlie's lips as he carried on talking about his family.

"How about Connor? That's your brother, right?"

"Yeah, he's great. We're not that close, though, but we get along well enough."

"Why aren't you close?"

"I don't know. I guess when I was young, I was always in my quiet corner drawing while he was out climbing trees with Rory or playing video games. We're not that far apart in age, but I suppose we just had different interests."

Hearing Charlie talk about his family really cemented in my mind what Charlie was worried about, and I promised myself that I wouldn't do anything that would put a strain on Charlie's relationship with his family. My sole goal was to keep Rory away and make sure Charlie enjoyed his sister's wedding just as he'd been looking forward to.

"So, when will I have a chance to meet this amazing family of yours?"

"There's a barbecue tomorrow for my family and some close friends, and in a couple of days is the rehearsal dinner."

"When's the wedding?"

"This weekend."

"So I still have you all to myself for the rest of the day."

Charlie didn't say anything, but he came close enough that I was able to put my arm around Charlie's shoulders and pull him even closer.

"Kris?"

"Yes?"

"You know how we kissed, well, a dozen times now?"

"I wasn't counting." I chuckled. "Go on…"

Charlie was trying so hard to hide his face from me, but it was pointless because I could see Charlie's flushed skin at the back of his neck, and damn if I didn't want to kiss it so bad.

"Are you…are we…is it going to happen again?"

"Would you like it to?"

"Yes," Charlie said, "very much."

We were close to the Old Mill but not close enough, so I pulled Charlie off the road by his hand

and didn't stop until we were surrounded by tall bushes.

I put my hands on either side of Charlie's face, placing a kiss on his cute button nose and taking some time looking at the little freckles under his eyes.

"Charlie, I need you to know that while our relationship may be fake, how I feel about touching you and kissing you isn't."

# 10

## CHARLIE

KRIS'S WORDS only half calmed me because, while it was true that I was worried about lying to my family or being found out, there was something else that worried me a lot more. Falling for Kris.

Kissing Kris felt right, more so than anyone I'd ever kissed before in my entire life.

When I was fifteen, I'd gone to an art gallery in New York with my aunt and uncle. They'd been looking to buy art for their new home and had brought me along because they knew I'd enjoy looking at all the paintings and drawings. They never found out how that visit changed how I saw life and love forever.

I'd roamed the walls of the gallery, sneaking photos of my favorite pieces with my cellphone, until

I saw a drawing on the wall that had captured my attention more than the rest. The pencil drawing had depicted the kiss between a man and a woman.

There wasn't much more than the outline of their faces and joined lips, but what I'd seen in the picture was the desire between two people, the connection, the love. It had been as though the picture was moving, and I could see the kiss in real-life three-dimensional Technicolor.

That day, fifteen-year-old me fell in love with the idea of being kissed the same way. I'd known I wouldn't be truly in love until I was kissed like that man and woman in the drawing.

I didn't have the opportunity until two years later when Rory stole my first kiss in my parent's kitchen on Christmas Day. It had been quick and had left me in shock because I'd always thought Rory was straight.

It had taken another six months of stolen kisses for our secret relationship to take off, but even though I'd thought I loved Rory, deep down I'd always known I wasn't in love with Rory. Our kisses had never made me feel the same way I'd imagined.

Now Kris's kisses, those made me feel that way and more. That's why I needed to set some ground rules now before I got my heart broken again.

"I can't sleep with you. I…I know I'm giving all the wrong signals, with having jumped you earlier and how hot our kisses were…because yes, well, they were hot, but it doesn't mean I want to…Crap, this is coming out all wrong. Shit." I turned away from Kris, feeling all kinds of embarrassed.

"Hey," Kris said, turning me around again, "that's okay. We don't have to do anything you don't want to." His voice was gentle and reassuring because of course he would be a good person on top of being the sexiest man I'd ever seen.

"Thanks, er…it's not that I don't want to, because I do…"

"You're afraid of how it may complicate things between us."

I nodded.

"I agree with you. God, Charlie, you're the easiest person to be around. You care about people and how your actions impact them. You have no idea how much that resonates with me." Kris ran his fingers through my hair. "You're also stupidly hot with your fiery red hair and those cute-as-fuck freckles."

I laughed. "You're making no sense."

"I know." Kris's eyes bore into me. "What I mean is that I will consciously need to stop myself from falling for you, so I agree that keeping things light will help us both."

"Because, in the end, you will go back to Lydovia and I will go back to Boston."

Kris paused for a moment but then nodded. "I hope I can still kiss you half stupid though. I mean, you already agreed to that, so no backing out now."

I sighed and leaned into Kris for a toe-curling kiss that got all those silly butterflies in my belly excited. I was going to be truly screwed, but fuck if I was willing to stop kissing Kris or able to find a good enough reason not to. I'd just need to deal with the fallback when I was back in Boston.

"Come on," Kris said. "You need to help me pick what to wear for your family's barbecue because my assistant picked all kinds of random things, and I have no clue what goes with what."

"You have an assistant?"

"What? No, no, I said my sister. She got me some clothes, but I haven't tried them, and I'm not that clued up on fashion. Will you help me?"

I wasn't sure why Kris had backtracked. Kris had clearly said it was his assistant that picked his clothes. He was obviously wealthy. Not that it bothered me at all or made me feel uncomfortable, but maybe Kris didn't want to seem to show off.

"I am just the man for the job," I said, pulling Kris in the direction of the Old Mill. "I mean, I'm no Tom Jones, but I still work in a men's fashion department."

"Tom Jones?"

"My roommate, he works with me in the store."

"Your roommate is called Tom Jones?"

"It's not unusual…"

Kris let out a belly laugh that gave me the giggles. We didn't stop until we reached the Old Mill. Olly was at the front, working on the flowers that adorned the entrance to the building.

"Hi, Olly. Still hard at work?" I asked.

"Oh no, it's not work when you get so much from it. Looking after the flowers is like spending all day with a friend. They don't much talk back at me, though." He smiled to himself. "And you? Have you had a good day? Hope you didn't meet Steve the swan on your walk by the river. He's not the friendliest."

"We met Charlie's aunt earlier. I'm sure that's why Steve kept away," Kris said, and I poked him in the ribs.

"Ouch…see, Olly? Maybe I need to see Steve for some protection."

I didn't miss the way Olly looked at both of us as he carried on working.

"These are purple wisteria; they symbolize good luck for the start of a business or marriage." He looked at Kris. "They're also good to express your affection after meeting someone for the first time." Then he looked at me. "See you later."

I smiled at Olly's random parting of information about his flowers.

"See you later, Olly," Kris said as we walked into the building holding hands. There was a tiny part of me that wanted to believe the meaning and significance of the flowers as we walked by the arch that would soon be covered in beautiful flowers.

———

I stopped before the point of no return. The receptionist at the local hotel had informed us that my family was all gathered at the back of the gardens in the barbecue area, so I cleaned my damp hands on the legs of my jeans, took a deep breath, and walked toward the doors that led to the gardens.

"Are you okay?" Kris asked.

I looked up at Kris and then at my family

through the glass panel of the double doors. "Yes, just a little nervous."

"Charlie, are you attracted to me?"

"What? Yes, you know that. Why are you asking?"

"Because I am very attracted to you."

I narrowed my eyes, not understanding what he meant.

"That's all they need to know about us. We're going to go out there, I'll charm the pants off everyone, and you can enjoy seeing your family."

"No pants off. That's a rule," I said.

"Really? Because that guy over there—"

I stopped Kris with a demanding kiss but had my tables turned on me when Kris pushed me against a nearby wall and covered my body with his, pressing us deliciously together.

"Fuck. You don't play fair," I said, struggling to draw a breath.

"Nope."

"Oh, Charlie, there you are."

I straightened at the sound of my mom's voice. She approached for a kiss, and I prayed she didn't notice I'd just been ravished within an inch of my sanity by one single kiss.

"Mom. Um, this is Kris. Kris, this is my mom, Caroline."

I stared as Kris took my mom's hand and placed a kiss on the back.

"It's a pleasure to meet you, Mrs. Williams."

"Oh, um…yes, same, I mean, nice to meet you. Please call me Caroline."

I rolled my eyes. Another woman in my family swooning over Kris. Not that I could blame them, Kris was very swoon-worthy.

"Shall we go check on the burned burgers, or have you warned the staff to keep Dad away from the barbecue?" I said.

"Your uncle is keeping him busy."

We walked out into the gardens where my family was gathered, some sitting on chairs, some on the ground, and some on picnic tables.

I couldn't remember the last time we'd all been together, so it was nice to look at them chatting away before they noticed us approaching.

Hannah was sitting cross-legged on a rug, having her blue and purple hair braided by Ellie. She looked so happy and relaxed.

"Is that Hannah?" Kris whispered in my ear.

"Yes, cover up your ears," I warned.

As predicted, when Hannah saw me, she screamed so loud dogs in Boston would have heard it. She got up and ran to me, jumping up and wrapping her legs around my waist, which caused me to nearly fall backward as I struggled to hold her.

"Ah, it runs in the family then." Kris chuckled next to me.

Hannah bounced back on her feet just as quickly. "So, you must be the Kris who got Aunt Gina's panties all wet. I can see why." She looked Kris up and down appreciatively.

Kris looked at me, confused.

"Don't mind her, it's all a pretense. She really doesn't care much for boys," I said.

"I really don't," Hannah said with a shrug. "I'm all about the girls."

"For the love of god, you two. It's like I raised a couple of savages."

"Sorry, Mom," we both said like we'd done so many times growing up, and then chuckled to each other.

"Nice to meet you, Kris," Hannah finally said, introducing herself. "I'm really happy you're joining Charlie for the wedding."

"Thank you for letting me barge in at the last minute."

Hannah waved her hand at Kris dismissively.

"Where's Connor? Has he arrived yet?" I asked.

Hannah frowned and looked around before she spoke.

"Something isn't right with Connor. He hasn't been around much lately."

"Is he here?"

Hannah nodded.

"On his own?"

"Sadly not. Anyway, I don't care about her. I just don't think Connor is well."

I'd seen Connor only four weeks ago when he'd had to go to Boston for work and had stayed with me. He'd seemed okay then, maybe a little tired, but I'd put it down to his new job.

"Have you spoken to him? You two have always been closer," I said.

Hannah was going to speak but then stopped herself when Rory approached us with a beer in hand.

"Hey, bridezilla," he said, kissing her cheek. "And who do we have here?"

"Rory, this is Kris, Charlie's boyfriend," Hannah said.

I felt Kris come closer and put one arm around my waist while he stretched the other to shake Rory's hand.

"Nice to meet you, Rory. You're Connor's best friend, right?" Kris asked, looking back at me for confirmation as though he didn't know exactly who Rory was.

"Yes…that's right," Rory said, his eyes boring into me as though they could burn through my skin.

I shivered from Kris's soft strokes on my back and felt myself leaning ever so slowly into him.

"How are you, Rory?" I asked, trying to be polite.

"I didn't realize you were seeing someone. Must be serious if you brought him to your sister's wedding."

I was lost for words. Not only was Rory publicly showing more interest in me than he ever had for fear of being outed, but he was also extremely rude talking about Kris as though he wasn't there.

"Baby"—I turned to Kris—"shall we grab a drink?"

"Thought you'd never ask," Kris replied, placing a kiss on the tip of my nose.

"Charlie, why don't we grab the drinks, and we can let Hannah get to know Kris better?" Rory said.

I was torn. I didn't want any alone time with Rory, and I didn't want to leave Kris's safe side, but I knew I'd need to get Rory to back off without an audience.

"I'll be right back," I said to Kris.

# 11

## KRIS

I DIDN'T WANT to let Charlie go with Rory, but I'd understood Charlie's silent message. He needed to do this on his own, to set things straight with Rory. As much as I wanted to be there for Charlie, I had to give him the space he needed.

"So, Kris, since I'm the bride—one of them, anyway—I'll let you buy me a drink so you can let me tell you all my brother's secrets."

I laughed. I was starting to really like Charlie's sister.

"Lead the way."

I was introduced to Charlie's dad, Martin, and his uncle, John, who were both within safe but commanding distance of the barbecue, making sure everyone got what they needed. Martin was a pleasant man, and I saw where Charlie got both his red hair and his personality from.

"Okay," Hannah said, "first of all, you need to know that if you hurt my little brother, I will cut your balls, I will cook them, and will make you eat them after. And you know what the worst part of that is?" She looked at me and paused for effect. "I'm a terrible cook."

I bit my lip, trying not to laugh. Hannah was so similar to Aleks I was pretty sure the two, if they met, would get on like a house on fire.

"I promise that I will only ever do what's best for Charlie. He's a great person, and I'm starting to see where he gets it from."

"Ooh, me?" Hannah clapped her hands together.

"Nope, your dad. I mean, look at him dying to get on the grill so he can make sure everyone has their food."

Hannah looked at me with a wide smile and bright green eyes, the same shade as Charlie's.

"We'll keep you. Now don't tell anyone, but I need another burger *and* another drink."

I laughed and told Hannah to join her fiancée and I'd get her some food and drink. I was looking forward to meeting Ellie and seeing what kind of woman it took to handle the bubbly firecracker that was Charlie's sister.

I didn't see Charlie and Rory anywhere near the drinks table. Not that I was expecting them to have their conversation where everyone would overhear.

Ellie was great, but I could only half pay attention to the conversation, so I stayed long enough to be polite before I excused myself to look for Charlie.

Charlie and Rory didn't seem to be anywhere I looked in the garden, so I decided to go inside the hotel to check if they were in the bar and that's when I heard a hushed conversation coming from the side of the building.

I approached carefully.

"Are you doing this to get back at me?" I overheard Rory's voice. He wasn't angry, but his tone was accusatory. I knew I shouldn't be listening but wanted to see how the conversation would play out and only intervene if necessary, so I leaned against the wall, trying to not get seen by Rory.

"What? No," Charlie said. "If you think I'd do that, then you don't know me at all."

"Then why is he here?"

"Because that's what people do, Rory. They bring their significant others to family weddings. It's called a plus one."

"You didn't have a plus one before," Rory said between gritted teeth.

"I do now, so…"

"And how about us?"

"Are you kidding me?" I heard the outrage in Charlie's voice and was proud that he was standing up for himself.

"We were together for almost three years, Charlie. Doesn't that mean anything?"

"That ended five years ago because you cheated on me repeatedly."

"You weren't around. I missed you and you weren't there."

Charlie let out a laugh. "And you thought the way to show me that you missed me was to sleep with other guys."

"I'm sorry, Charlie. I've changed. We've known each other for years. Can't you give us another chance?"

Charlie paused, and I felt my heart was on my hands. Whatever Charlie said next could change everything.

"Rory, even if I still had feelings for you, which I don't, we still wouldn't get back together because I'm not going to spend my life hiding. It wouldn't be fair on me or my family. Only you can decide when to come out, and I would never make you do that, but I am not the person for you."

"And he is?" Rory's voice was more agitated, so I got ready to intervene.

"I don't owe you any explanations about my relationship or anything else."

"And how about our kiss?"

I decided then that Charlie and Rory's conversation was over. I didn't care about anything that had happened between them before I met Charlie, but I also didn't want to hear it.

I stepped out from my hiding place and bumped into Charlie almost straight away. He tensed but then wrapped his arms around me.

"Hey, you okay? You were gone ages, so I came to find you," I said, looking around for Rory, but he was gone.

"Yes, I'm okay. He doesn't get it, but he thinks we're together, so he'll leave me alone."

"That's good."

I kissed Charlie, savoring the softness of his lips.

"Damn, you kiss so good," Charlie said against my lips.

"Ditto."

We both laughed.

"Shall we go back to your family? Your sister was going to tell me a story about crayons."

Charlie rested his head against my chest.

"It's not that funny."

"What isn't?"

"The crayon story."

"Well, now because you're saying that, I definitely need to hear it." I placed another kiss on Charlie's lips. "Because I'm pretty sure the truth will be somewhere between your version and Hannah's, but I bet hers is more entertaining."

Charlie groaned. "Fine. Just remember we didn't agree to this so you could witness my humiliation at the hands of my family."

Charlie's family was great. While I hadn't yet met Charlie's brother, the rest of the family had been nothing short of welcoming, considering up until twenty-four hours ago they hadn't even known about my existence.

Through their stories, I found out how cute Charlie had been as a kid and how his passion for drawing had started, Hannah's first hair dye experiment, and how great Connor had been at sports.

I'd listened and taken it all in. My experience of family gatherings was so different from Charlie's. No less loving, just different.

We were sitting on the grass with Charlie's back leaning against my front as he drew on his sketchpad. Every so often, I placed little butterfly kisses on the back of his neck and watched as the little hairs stood up. That was clearly a sensitive area for Charlie, something I made a mental note of.

From my privileged point of view, I was able to see Charlie at work. I looked around and saw no one had noticed that Charlie was drawing, or maybe they were just so used to it, they didn't pay attention to it anymore.

Charlie had kept his side of the conversation going without ever stopping what he was doing. Everyone talked, ate, and drank. Charlie drew. Ellie's hands were on Hannah's hair, Charlie's dad looked adoringly at his wife, and John massaged Gina's hands as she chatted away with Hannah.

I wondered what Charlie would draw if he was able to look back at us from a distance. Did we look good together? Because it sure felt good being there with Charlie among the family.

My cellphone buzzed in my pocket. I'd almost forgotten I had it with me because the signal had been so patchy in Chester Falls.

Charlie kissed my cheek before I got up to take the call. He looked relaxed and happy. For a moment,

I cursed my phone for taking me away from Charlie, but I'd looked at the caller ID and seen Aleks's name, so I knew I needed to take the call.

"Hey, Sestra," I said, using the nickname I dedicated for her only when I was away from home. I walked back into the building and went straight for the bar, which was empty due to the early hour, and sat on one of the stools.

"Kris, for the love of god, are you okay? I've been calling you for days, and your cellphone is always off." Aleks's voice was laced with worry.

"Yes, I'm okay. I couldn't stay with James because someone alerted the press. I'm staying somewhere safe, but the cell connection is very poor. I'm sorry I've made you worry. It wasn't my intention."

I heard Aleks exhale on the other end of the line.

"Are you sure it's safe? What if someone recognizes you?"

"I'm in the last place anyone would think of finding the prince of Lydovia, Sestra. Don't worry, the press won't know where I am."

"Kris, it's not just about the press. It's your safety too. Where's James?"

"He's with me, don't worry." I didn't feel good about lying, but I didn't want to worry my sister. "I have to go, Aleks. I'll do better to keep in touch."

"Wait…Kris, there was a reason I was trying to reach you. Papa isn't well. He's seen the royal physician and had some tests. I'm worried about his health."

"I'll come home," I said. The news of my father's poor health took me by surprise. The king had always been the strong head of the family, running the country with the energy and tenacity of someone half his age. Not that he was old, by any means, since he was only in his mid-sixties.

My stomach sank when I realized I'd miss Hannah's wedding and I'd be leaving Charlie on his own literally hours after being introduced to his family.

"No, that's not necessary. I just wanted you to know. You know how the king is. He's likely working into the night when we all think he's asleep. I'll call you if something changes."

"Thanks, Sestra. Love you."

"Love you, too, Brat."

I stared at my phone after terminating the call.

"Difficult conversation?"

I looked up to see I wasn't alone in the bar anymore. A tall, slim woman was sitting a few stools away cradling a drink. How had I missed her coming in and getting served?

"Um, yeah."

"Let me know if you want to borrow a friendly ear. Sometimes it's easier to talk to strangers." Her tone was somewhere between friendly and flirty.

"I'm good. Thanks anyway."

She stretched out her hand. "Ceecee Bloomfield. Are you staying here?"

"Kris…um, just Kris. No, I'm here for an event."

Her face changed immediately. "Oh, the wedding," she said with a bitter tone to her voice. "Maybe see you around, just Kris." She got up and headed in the direction of the rooms.

I waited until Ceecee was out of sight and picked up my cellphone again. This time, I dialed James's number.

"Kris. I was just about to call you."

"You got told off by Her Royal Highness too?" I chuckled.

"I was, indeed. But I was still going to call you. The press has gone away. When shall I pick you up?"

"Oh, how did you manage that?"

"I had a famous friend pop by. They got some photos of her walking her dogs and decided there was nothing to see here and left."

"That's great. I need a favor. Two, actually."

"Go on."

"I need you to promise you'll keep this to yourself."

James took a deep sigh as though he already knew I was going to ask something he wasn't sure he should do.

"I met someone."

"Kris…"

"It's not what you're thinking, James. I really like him, but nothing is going to happen. I just need you to keep an eye on the Falls Hotel. I'm going to attend a small wedding here this weekend, so I need you around in case the press turns up."

"Okay, I'll head over there tonight. What's the other thing?"

"Can you do a check on someone called Ceecee Bloomfield?"

"Are you serious?" James asked.

"Yeah. Why, do you recognize the name?"

"Kris, Ceecee Bloomfield is THE fucking press."

# 12

## CHARLIE

Since Kris had got up to answer his cellphone, I thought I'd check in on Connor. I wasn't surprised to hear his girlfriend, who Hannah and I named Wicked Witch, had wanted to stay at the hotel instead of at my parents' in Connor's old room.

I noticed Kris at the bar on the way up to the rooms. Once I'd seen Connor, we could head back to the Old Mill. I wondered if Kris would be up for a relaxing evening watching old movies. I didn't want to monopolize Kris's time, but there was a part of me that also wanted to be with Kris as long as possible. I mean, if we were going to pass as a couple, we'd need to spend some time together, right?

Connor looked like death warmed over when he answered the door.

"Con." I didn't even know what to say.

"Hey, Charlie, come in." Connor let me in and went to sit on the bed. It looked like he'd been sleeping when I'd knocked.

I sat on a nearby chair and took a good look at my older brother. He had bags under his eyes and looked too pale. Connor had almost always had a tan because of the amount of time he spent playing sports outdoors. This Connor looked paler than me. How was that possible?

"Are you ill?" I asked.

"What? No, I'm just tired."

Connor picked up his cellphone from the side table, looked at it with a frown, and put it back down.

"Is everything okay with you? Whatever it is, you can talk to me, Con."

Connor stared at me for a moment and then looked away.

"There are a few things going on. Work wants me to lay off twenty people. I know it's a test. They have three people competing to manage the biggest project the company has ever landed, and we all have different tasks to do, but mine is the only one that directly affects people and their livelihood." Connor rubbed his eyes. "I can't find a way around it."

"What does your gut feeling tell you?" That was the question Connor always asked me whenever I had doubts about anything, from going to art school to staying in Boston despite the lack of job opportunities.

Connor laughed. "My gut tells me I don't want to work for a company that puts their profit ahead of the people that have been making that profit for over ten years."

We locked eyes and I smiled.

"It's easier said than done. I'm not like you, Charlie. You were always so brave, never afraid to be yourself and go for what you wanted."

I gawked at my brother. "Are you serious? You were mister popular all throughout school. Life couldn't have been easier for you."

"Not everything was as it looked."

I was going to ask what he meant, but Connor said the Wicked Witch—well, he didn't quite call her that—was arriving shortly, so he wanted to catch a shower before she got there. The conversation wasn't over as far as I was concerned.

Connor was struggling with something personal. Maybe his relationship had hit a rocky place, or maybe it was something else. Whatever it was, I wanted to be there for him like he'd been for me so many times in the past despite our differences.

Kris was talking to Aunt Gina when I got back out to the gardens, but as soon as he saw me, he strode over and picked me up, planting a kiss right smack on the lips.

"What was that for?" I asked, giggling.

"Do I need a reason to kiss my boyfriend?"

My heart skipped a beat. God, did I ever want that to be true, for us to be boyfriends for real and not just pretending. Were our kisses even pretend anymore? They certainly didn't feel that way.

"Do you want to get back to the apartments and have a movie night?" I asked.

"A movie night?"

"It's an evening when one or more people sit around in their pajamas watching movies and eating bad food until they can't keep their eyes open."

Kris pulled me closer and whispered in my ear, "I don't have any pajamas. I sleep naked."

My cock went from interested to full mast within seconds. Kris's breath on my ear, his voice, and especially what he'd said was enough to make me feel like I could either melt in a puddle at his feet or spontaneously combust.

"I…um… Kris, fuck, you're killing me here."

"Me?" Kris said in the sweetest, most innocent voice while batting his eyelashes.

I shook my head, hearing Hannah whistling at us from where she was sitting.

We took a cab back to the apartment, stopping at the store to buy snacks.

"I vote for your apartment since you have a bigger TV," I said before going into my apartment to prepare the popcorn and change into sweats and a T-shirt.

I knocked on Kris's door ten minutes later.

"It's open," I heard Kris shout from inside.

I turned the door handle and used my hip to prop the door open while I went in. I froze and nearly dropped the popcorn bowl. Kris was sitting on the bed under the covers and his chest was bare, which led me to believe he was fully naked. I mean, he did say he didn't have any pajamas. I'd thought he was joking at the time, maybe not after all.

I swallowed, my mouth feeling suddenly too dry. At the gym, I'd avoided looking at Kris, but there was nothing I could do now. I was staring right at the very defined muscles on Kris's body, at the dark hair of his chest that happily trailed down to…to…*fuck*.

"Why are you naked?" I squeaked.

Kris narrowed his eyes. "I'm not naked. I have

boxer shorts on, look." He uncovered his lower half, and I instinctively closed my eyes.

"Oh, dear god, why do you do this to me? Did I do something to piss you off? I mean, I know it was naughty pretending I had that doctor's appointment so I didn't have to cover that weekend shift two months ago, but come on," I rambled to no one.

"Charlie?"

I opened one eye. "Yes?"

"Does this make you uncomfortable?" Kris sounded worried.

"No…no. It's just you're so, well, have you looked at yourself in the mirror?"

Kris laughed.

I leaned back on the closed door, holding onto the popcorn bowl like it was a life raft.

"Are we doing this movie night thing?" Kris asked, one eyebrow quirked.

When I didn't move, Kris got up from the bed and came toward me. He took the popcorn bowl with one hand, locked the door behind me, and pulled me toward the bed.

My heart was beating off my chest. I wanted Kris so badly, but I was afraid that if I did, things wouldn't stop there, and it was getting harder and harder to resist temptation. No pun intended.

"Charlie, we don't have to do anything. It's a warm night so let's just get comfortable and watch a movie, okay?"

I nodded and let out a breath.

"God, Kris, do you have any idea how much I want you?"

Kris touched my cheek with the backs of his fingers and then ran his thumb over my lips.

"Yes. Yes, I do, because I feel the exact same way."

I wrapped my arms around Kris's shoulders, feeling the warmth of his skin. Our lips met like they had a few times before, but also in a new way. There was no rush to dominate, no pretense for anyone else. It was just me and Kris.

As our tongues played with each other, stealing a taste, I knew that whoever Kris was outside of Chester Falls, it didn't matter, much like it didn't matter that I was nothing more than a store manager with dreams of capturing the world around me on paper.

When we parted, I removed my clothes and took my place on the bed next to Kris.

"Which movie are we watching?" I asked.

"*Cinema Paradiso*. It's an Italian movie."

"I've never seen it. What is it about?"

"It's about many things. Friendship, love—mostly

the kind of love that never goes away, even when people can't be together, it's still there under the surface just waiting for the right moment to come out again."

I looked at Kris. His eyes were shiny and a little sad.

"Tell me why this is your favorite movie," I said, and Kris looked at me, surprised.

"How did you know it's my favorite?"

"Your eyes, and the way you described it."

We both leaned back on the headboard, and I let Kris pull me closer so my back was against his chest. It was warm, strong, and safe.

"The first time I watched it, I was quite young. It was my mother's favorite movie. I liked the music, so I practiced the piano all the time until I could play it for her. She died when I was eleven."

Seeing Kris choked up broke my heart. "Oh, Kris, I'm so sorry. I can't even…" All I could do was offer some comfort now and listen to the story with the understanding he was sharing something really precious with me.

"I couldn't bear to watch it for years. I was sixteen when, one day, it was playing on TV, and I just couldn't look away or change the channel. Somehow, I found myself watching it with a brand-new pair of eyes because I'd grown up and finally understood what she saw in the movie."

"What was that?"

"That life is about laughing, being silly, being a friend, fighting for what you want, and most of all, it's about love, the kind that makes you do silly things but that will always live."

I turned around in Kris's arms, trying to keep in the few tears that were trying to escape. "That's the most beautiful thing I've ever heard."

Kris smiled and pressed Play.

I struggled with the subtitles at first because the movie was in Italian, but once I got used to it, I got into the story, and just as Kris had described, the movie had been about all those things. I wondered if Kris had ever known feelings so strong or if he was still searching. Maybe the movie was to Kris what that drawing at the gallery had been to me, the representation of the perfect connection between two people.

At some point during the movie, we'd shifted positions so we were lying down more than sitting, and when the credits rolled, Kris turned the TV off and pulled me closer.

"Please stay."

"Okay."

I kissed him gently and settled against him.

We'd had a perfect day, and I'd let myself believe for a moment that I had a life with Kris and that it would always be like this.

But even as I was falling asleep more content than I'd ever felt before, I thought that real life wasn't a drawing, and it certainly wasn't a movie. It would only be a matter of time until the other shoe dropped.

# 13

## KRIS

WHEN I OPENED MY EYES, the first thing I saw was bright red hair shining in the morning sun that came through the windows despite the heavy rain outside.

Charlie was lying half on top of me, and all I could think was how perfect it was to have him there. Why couldn't we do this all the time, forever?

Oh yeah, because I was a prince with a whole load of responsibilities, not enough freedom, and there was no way I'd ever wish my life on someone as ingenuous as Charlie. The press would eat him up and spit him out without mercy. After all, that's what they'd tried to do to Sergei when we'd first come out as a couple.

Initially, it had been very tough, but Sergei had grown up in the royal household. He knew the rules of play, so he'd fought back and showed them all he was worthy of being with the prince.

None of that mattered, because once Hannah and Ellie's wedding was over, Charlie would go home, and I would stay at Chester Falls or go back to James's place until it was time for the president's ball, and then I'd go home, too, and slot into the mold I was expected to fit in.

I'd been on the phone to James as soon as we'd come back to the apartment the night before while Charlie had got the popcorn for our movie night. It had been a tense conversation because James still hadn't been able to figure out why Ceecee Bloomfield was in the area, and especially at the hotel Charlie's family had booked out almost entirely.

The only thing I could do was stay close to the apartment for as long as possible and only leave for the rehearsal dinner with Charlie. James had agreed to serve as our cab driver to the venue so he could keep an eye and let me know if he saw Ceecee.

Charlie stirred, and I held my breath, waiting for a reaction. We'd had a great time at the barbecue, and our movie night had ended perfectly, but now, in the light of day, I wasn't sure if things would suddenly feel awkward.

Charlie's sleepy, light-green eyes looked like precious jewels when he looked up. I touched his cheek, feeling the short stubble. Relief washed over me when he smiled. Not just any old smile, but the smile of someone who was happy to be exactly where he was.

"Morning," Charlie said.

"Come here." I pulled him in for a kiss, but he hid his face under my chin.

"Ugh, morning breath."

I chuckled. "Don't care, kiss me already." And so he did, a slow, languid kiss that made my toes curl and perk my morning wood up even more than it already was.

Charlie moaned against my lips, and I swallowed every single one of them. I tightened my hold on Charlie's waist to stop myself from flipping him over and pressing him down into the mattress.

It had been a while since I'd had any kind of sex that didn't involve my hand, so having Charlie grinding against me was both the best thing ever and pure torture.

"It's raining," Charlie said as he released my lips and carried on kissing and sucking on my jaw and all the way down my neck, biting my Adam's apple before trailing a path down my chest.

"Yes, it is." I choked. "Charlie, baby, you need to stop that."

Charlie stopped but didn't move. His mouth was perilously close to one of my nipples while his hand was teasing the other. I'd always been very sensitive there, so I knew I needed to check Charlie was okay to continue what we were doing before I gave in to this intense need that was consuming me.

"You don't want this?" Charlie asked, his warm breath ghosting over my nipple, causing me to shiver.

I touched Charlie's cheek and leaned down for a kiss. "Baby, it scares me how much I want it."

Charlie lay back on his pillow and exhaled. "I'm sorry. I got carried away."

I didn't want Charlie to be sorry or to stop what he was doing, but we'd had an agreement, and for Charlie, I wouldn't push to break that agreement. Even if it felt like he was ready to break it himself.

Charlie got up and went over to the window. I followed him and put my arms around his waist from behind, admiring his milky, white skin, so smooth and filled with freckles.

Charlie leaned his head back on my shoulder. "I always liked the rain. I used to think the reason it rained was so everyone had a chance to do something wild, different, and it would never be found because the noise of the rain drowned everything and then washed the evidence away."

"That's a nice thought. Have you ever done something wild or different under the shelter of the rain?" I asked.

"Connor left his bike outside once, so I rode it in the rain and got it all muddy. I'd left the bike outside so by the time the rain stopped it was all clean again."

I smiled against the skin of Charlie's shoulder. "Anything else?"

He chuckled. "I used to steal cookies from the cookie jar and take them up to my room so I could eat them while I watched the rain outside. I didn't think anyone knew until I realized the cookie jar always had my favorite cookies in it, not Hannah's or Connor's."

I wanted to comment on Charlie's story. Say something funny or just state that his cookie story was the cutest thing I'd ever heard, but my vocal cords had seized. There was something stuck in my throat, and I was terrified I'd let it out because I could never un-say it.

I would have to keep it in and take it back to Lydovia because there was no way I'd burden Charlie with the knowledge that I had without a shadow of a doubt fallen for him.

Charlie turned around and looked at me. His eyes were searching, almost as though he knew something monumental had changed.

I took Charlie's mouth and devoured it like it was my last meal, hoping that the carnal exploration masked the whirlpool of feelings I was both trying to convey and hide.

"Let's go for a walk before breakfast," Charlie suggested. "I think we both need the fresh air, and who knows, maybe we'll get to do something wild." He winked.

Charlie went to his room to grab some clean clothes before we met again outside the apartments. We smiled at each other when Charlie opened his door.

"Man, I'm losing my touch," I joked when Charlie failed to bump into me again.

"If you want me to fall all over you, you have to buy me breakfast first."

"Again? I knew you were with me for the money." I shook my head in mock seriousness, and Charlie gave me a light punch in the stomach.

"Hey, I've worked hard for these." I lifted my T-shirt, showing my defined abs, and Charlie pretended to faint.

This was good. Our easy flirting and making jokes at each other's expense was a good place to be.

I took Charlie's hand and led him downstairs. The smell of coffee from the guys who were working in the building made us change our mind and go for our rainy walk after eating first.

Benny wasn't at the diner. Instead, a woman with wiry, white hair tied in a bun on top of her head greeted us.

"Charlie, my gorgeous boy. Benny said you were around, and I didn't believe him."

She put her arms around Charlie who hugged her back.

"Momma Ruth, this is Kris my em...boyfriend," he said shyly.

"Oh my." Momma Ruth fanned herself, and I saw Charlie roll his eyes from the corner of mine.

"It's a pleasure to meet you, ma'am," I said and took her hand for a kiss.

Benny came through the door and rushed to grab his wife's hand from me and took her to the kitchen. Charlie pulled me toward a table, and I looked behind us to see Benny planting a very energetic kiss on Momma Ruth's lips.

"Go Benny." I chuckled.

"You know, with great looks comes great responsibility."

I smiled at the stolen quote and picked a menu from the table.

"Have you ever had pumpkin spice pancakes?"

"Had what?"

"Trust me with your breakfast?" Charlie asked.

"If you can get Benny to let go of Momma Ruth, I'll be impressed enough to eat anything you put in front of me," I said.

Charlie straightened his back and put on a determined face before he called Momma Ruth.

"Momma, would you be able to fix us with your special pumpkin spice pancakes?"

"You know I don't have them out of season, Charlie," she said, although something told me it wasn't quite true.

"I do know." Charlie maintained eye contact with her until she broke into a smile.

"Coming right up, you little devil. I'll get you some coffee too."

"Do you think my puppy eyes worked?" Charlie asked.

"They'd work for me any time, baby."

Charlie looked down at the table and blushed.

When breakfast came, we both laughed at the

enormous portion of pancakes. The scent of cinnamon, nutmeg, and ginger wafting from the pancakes reminded me of Christmas at home and Mimi's winter cakes.

"These are delicious," I said, running a portion over the syrup before bringing it to my mouth, careful not to drip the syrup all over my clothes.

"We used to have them for breakfast on the weekend growing up. It was so messy." Charlie laughed. "Did you have any family traditions like that growing up?"

I thought about it.

"Yes. My parents often had to attend evening events, so I remember my mom reading us bedtime stories while all dressed up to go out. She always looked so beautiful."

"What does your dad do for a living?"

I froze. I should have kept my mouth shut, but I was so comfortable with Charlie it was easy to forget no one was meant to know who I was, and now it was more for Charlie's safety than my own, because if we were caught together, it would start a whole new shitstorm I didn't want Charlie involved in.

"Um, he's in public service."

Charlie nodded, seemingly satisfied with the white lie. Suddenly, I wasn't hungry anymore.

"Shall we go on our wet walk?" I suggested, hoping the change would bring on new topics of conversation.

"Absolutely."

Just as Charlie spoke, Olly came into the diner.

"Hi, Olly," I said.

"Hey, boys, going for a walk in this weather?"

"You probably think we're crazy," Charlie said.

Olly pointed at the stack of umbrellas by the door of the diner. "Most people don't know what they're missing out on by staying away from the rain," he said. "This weather is also good to plant seeds because you don't need to worry about watering them."

My hand went instinctively to my jeans pocket. The small bag with seeds that Olly had given me was there. I could have sworn I'd put them on top of my suitcase the other day.

## 14

---

## CHARLIE

I INHALED DEEPLY as we joined the path by the river. I loved the smell of rain, that earthy scent that made me feel like I was part of the world around me.

God, it really made me miss home. I regretted that not wanting to bump into Rory had kept me away from home, not just from my family, because they often traveled into Boston to visit, but home. The house I grew up in, the big yard, the long walks I loved to do in the field at the back of the house. I even missed my old neighbors, Mr. and Mrs. Clarke, who were more like surrogate grandparents.

The rain wasn't as heavy as it had been when we'd woken up earlier, but it was still persistent, so I put my arm through Kris's as he held the umbrella.

"What's the weather like in Lydovia?"

"It's perfect," Kris said. "Despite global warming, we still have four distinct seasons, and we have mountains that have snow all year round on their peaks. I think you'd like it there. Lots of things to draw."

I looked up at Kris to find his gaze on me. I couldn't read his eyes, but they looked regretful, almost sad.

"Maybe one day I can visit. Will you show me around?"

Kris smiled and nodded.

"Where would you take me?"

"I would show you the botanical gardens, the waterfall, my favorite lake, and especially the trail in the woods that no one knows about that leads to the most beautiful meadow you could ever imagine. It's magical in the spring, like you're swimming in a sea of flowers."

"Sounds beautiful."

"It is."

We walked in silence for a while with me never letting go of Kris's arm. I thought about the night before and waking up in Kris's arms this morning. It had been perfect until I'd got lost in Kris's lips and the rest of my brain function had gone out the window.

It was a good thing Kris had been stronger than

me and had stopped it before we went too far. Not that I would regret it. I was starting to believe that the self-imposed boundary wouldn't do a damned thing when it came to Kris. Whether I wanted or not, I was falling for Kris hard and fast.

The gravelly patch was crunchy under our feet, and the sounds of the raindrops on the umbrella all made me think of a different season when all the leaves on the trees went a golden shade of brown before they fell.

The rainfall increased, so Kris put his arm around me to protect me from the cold showers, especially as it seemed that with Kris's height advantage, I was getting more of the rain on me.

Not that I minded, it was only water after all. Our little patch of the world was being washed, and it would dry again soon.

That thought took me back to the conversation we'd had earlier about the rain, and suddenly my body had a mind of its own as I took Kris's hand and pulled him away from the graveled path toward a big tree that was a few yards away and partially hidden by tall vegetation.

My hair was stuck to my forehead and dripping down my face. My shirt was getting soaked, but my skin was scorching so the cold rain was actually welcome.

"Charlie, what—" Kris didn't have time to say any more before I pushed him against the tree and pulled his head down for a kiss.

Kris responded immediately, giving my tongue permission to explore his mouth. He tasted of coffee and pumpkin spice, my two favorite flavors, and I loved every lick, every taste, every bite.

The kiss wasn't enough and soon my hands roamed down Kris's chest, feeling all the hard bumps of his abdominal muscles contracting under my touch and giving me the confidence to continue my exploration.

The umbrella was on the ground. Thank goodness Kris had had the good sense of closing it to stop it from flying away because I couldn't care less about anything but the man under my touch.

I'd felt Kris's erection that morning when we were only in our boxer shorts, but I hadn't had a chance to touch it. I wasn't going to let anything stop me this time, not unless Kris really wanted me to stop, but considering how he was struggling to draw a breath and had leaned his head back on the tree, it was an unlikely event.

"Charlie... Jesus, fuck..."

"Kris, please don't make me stop." I pulled Kris's T-shirt up, revealing the hard peaks of his nipples. I was grinding against him, trying to find some relief, but our clothes were in the way.

I licked and sucked, paying attention to one nipple and then the other. His chest hair was soft, his body hard, and I just wanted to touch him everywhere. Kris's hands came around the back of my neck to keep me in place. When I bit one of his nipples, Kris let out a guttural groan, and suddenly, I was the one with my back against the tree.

"I don't want to stop, baby," Kris said against my mouth. It was his turn to explore my clothed body, reaching farther south than I had on him.

"Please, Kris…more. I need more." More kisses, more of his touch, more of Kris. I needed everything. Was it even still raining? Who the fuck knew because Kris's hands pressing on my hard cock was making my blood rush all over my body so quickly I almost felt lightheaded.

"Charlie." Kris's voice was soft but assertive. I hadn't even realized I'd closed my eyes, but as soon as Kris spoke, I opened them to stare at the dark depths of Kris's gaze. He focused on my eyes as though he was searching for answers to a question he hadn't asked. Whatever it was, I knew what the answer was.

"Yes."

Kris chuckled.

"Was it true? What you said earlier?"

"About what?"

"What happens in the rain?"

"Yes," was all I said before fisting my hands on Kris's shirt and going for another kiss. Between his body heat and how I was feeling inside, I was surprised I hadn't combusted yet despite the cool rain.

"I want to taste you," Kris said before he gave me a last soft kiss, got on his knees, and unbuttoned my jeans. He only pulled them down enough to take my already-leaking cock out.

The relief of having my erection free from the trap of the wet jeans was short lived when Kris took my cock in his mouth and sucked my crown. My knees nearly gave way under the pleasure, and I had to place my hands on Kris's shoulders to keep upright.

One of Kris's hands wrapped around my cock, twisting deliciously, and adding pressure that, with the additional sucking of the head, was getting me close to blowing. The other hand taking turns massaging my ass and tugging on my balls.

"Oh god, Kris...ngn..." I brought one hand up

to my mouth and bit hard to stop myself from being too loud in case there were any curious passers-by.

When I felt myself engulfed in the heat of Kris's mouth all the way down to the root, I couldn't hold it any longer. I came so hard I had to place my hand back on Kris's shoulders or I'd have been a messy gooey puddle of pleasure on the ground.

Kris stood and embraced me, kissing me reverently as though I'd just given him the best gift ever, and not the other way around.

I allowed Kris to command the kissing while I recovered from my earth-shattering orgasm, but as soon as I could think with the correct head again, I went for Kris's jeans.

They were soaking wet, which made them hard to open. Just as Kris had done, I only pushed the jeans down enough that I had room to play. Kris was long and thick, and I wondered how amazing it would feel to have him inside me. Despite having just orgasmed, my hole clenched at the thought.

It wasn't something that would happen today, or maybe ever, so I decided to focus on what I'd been dying to do all day, have a taste.

I went down on my knees and replaced my hand with my mouth.

"Holy mother of—" Kris swore. My chest

expanded at the thought that I was the one respon-sible for unraveling the tall, sexy man in front of me. I changed my position so I could look up at Kris and found him looking back, his mouth slightly open and his eyelids half closed.

I hummed my pleasure at the musky, salty taste. Unfortunately, I couldn't take all of his cock, so I'd had to use my hand, choosing instead to focus on the purple head. When I reached farther into his jeans to tug on his balls, he came in my mouth with the best sound of pleasure and abandon I'd ever heard.

Kris slid down the tree and sat on the wet ground. It was still raining, and we were now soaked to the bone. I straddled Kris and then kissed him, pulling the dark wet hair away from his forehead. Kris looked as thoroughly debauched as I felt. We both laughed.

"Come on, we should go back and change into dry clothes," Kris said as he ran his hand up and down my back, making me shiver. The awareness of the cold rain was starting to settle in. I knew the rain would wash away all the evidence of what we'd done, and soon we'd both be in dry, clean clothes. This would be just a memory, a dream, the one time we both gave in before everything was reset back to how it was.

Before we got up, Kris reached for the pocket of

his jeans and took out a small bag of seeds. He gazed into my eyes, and without breaking eye contact he put half the seeds in my hand, and together, we spread them around us until there were none left.

The walk back to the apartments was in silence, but not silent because my mind was loud and working overtime, wondering what would happen now and if this had changed things between us. So much for the rain washing it all away. I laughed.

"What's up?" Kris asked, pulling me closer to keep me warm as we walked.

"Nothing, just...nothing." I sighed.

Kris kissed the side of my head. "Didn't really work for you either, did it?"

"What didn't?"

"The rain. It didn't wash it away."

"No," I admitted quietly.

"I don't want it to. I want to remember this forever so I can carry it with me everywhere I go."

"Oh, Kris, don't say stuff like that. You're making it really hard."

"I'm sorry, baby."

We decided it was best to go to our separate apartments for a shower, but Kris had asked me to come back to his apartment using the connecting door and to bring my bigger sketchpad.

I wanted to punch the tiled wall of the shower in frustration. I didn't know how to tell Kris that I wanted more than the days we had in Chester Falls. Why couldn't we date? Some long-distance relationships worked, right?

I thought about what I knew about Kris, and it wasn't much. It dawned on me that while I'd talked a lot about myself, my work, my passion for drawing, and had introduced my family due to our plan to avoid Rory, Kris hadn't said more than the reason he was in Chester Falls.

Kris had talked a little about his family but not much about his dad. Were they estranged?

Part of me wanted to focus on the missing information as a way to find a fault in Kris so it would make it easier to put some distance between us. Then again, I'd looked into his eyes as he'd spoken about his mom's favorite movie the night before. Those feelings had been real, and then Kris had asked me to stay the night as though he really needed me there.

There wasn't much I could do, so I finished my shower, dried off, and picked some tracksuit bottoms and a T-shirt to wear.

I knocked on the connecting door before opening it, smiling at the thought I'd had when I first came to the apartment, wondering if I'd have a noisy neighbor.

When I went inside Kris's room, I noticed a tray with fresh coffee and cookies from Benny's. My stomach rumbled at the sight of the snack, and I was dying for a coffee, so I went over to the tray and poured the coffee into the two empty cups.

Kris came out of the bathroom wearing nothing but a towel around his hips, and his hair was messy from the shower. He smiled and went to his suitcase to grab some clothes. I kept busy serving the coffee to avoid looking in Kris's direction.

When I knew Kris was fully clothed, I turned around to give him his drink, and that's when I noticed the large mirror that was propped onto two chairs facing the bed.

## 15

## KRIS

CHARLIE STARED at the mirror and then looked at me.

"What's the mirror for?" he asked.

"Do you remember when I asked you to draw me? I changed my mind."

He looked disappointed so I clarified.

"I want you to draw us. Come," I said, coaxing Charlie toward the bed.

"Us?"

"Yes."

I took the coffee mug from Charlie's hand and placed it on the side table. I sat on the bed against the headboard and pulled Charlie to sit between my legs. The way we were sitting with the mirror slightly on the side meant Charlie had a good view of our profile rather than looking straight on.

I reached out for the sketchpad and placed it on Charlie's lap.

Our eyes met in the mirror and time stopped. This was what I'd imagined when Charlie was sketching his family at the barbecue. I'd known without even seeing then that we'd fit together so perfectly it was almost painful to think of us not being together both on paper and in real life.

Charlie picked up his pencils and started drawing.

I didn't want to look until the drawing was finished, so I broke one of the cookies into small pieces and fed them to Charlie, drank my own coffee, and mostly just stared at our joined reflection in the mirror.

Charlie shivered when I sat back a little and ran my hand over his back, placing small butterfly kisses all the way up and then on the back of his neck. The small light hairs on Charlie's neck stood up under the soft touch of my lips.

"Sorry, I didn't mean to distract you," I said when Charlie paused. He had his eyes closed and his head tilted to give me better access.

"Then you'll need to stop doing that."

"Noted."

I resumed my appreciation of our reflection, focusing on Charlie's look of concentration. I let my mind wander to places I probably shouldn't but decided to indulge for a few minutes.

Would Charlie like Lydovia? I was convinced he would. Charlie was a country person at heart despite living in the city. I imagined a life where he would spend his days drawing and the nights in my bed. A life where we'd attend events together and work with the charities we were passionate about.

It could happen, right?

"It's ready."

"Yes…sorry, what?" I stuttered as my mind came back into focus.

"The drawing is ready. Do you want to see it?" Charlie held the sketch against his chest like he was terrified to show it.

"Please."

My voice became trapped in my throat when Charlie revealed the drawing. I'd thought Charlie would draw our figures together with Charlie sitting back against my chest on the bed.

Instead, he'd drawn our heads and shoulders as if we were locked in an embrace. My head came over Charlie's shoulder, with my eyes closed and a smile that captured everything I was feeling. Charlie was looking down and only part of his face was drawn, the rest faded out until it blended with the white paper, but I could see it was Charlie. He had a tiny beauty mark under his right eye. His eyes were open and looking down, but despite it being a pencil drawing, I could swear I saw the real green color of Charlie's eyes.

"Charlie." I choked. "This is the second most beautiful thing I've ever seen."

"Second?" Charlie laughed, although it came out more like he had something trapped in his chest.

"The real you is the most beautiful thing I've ever seen."

I took the sketchpad and placed it on the side table, then I pushed Charlie down on the bed and kissed him. We made out for the longest time, no words exchanged, just light touches, some hot and heavy kissing, and some soft pecks. We lay on the bed side by side, staring at each other until his cellphone went off.

"What's that?" Charlie asked, still looking dazed from our make-out session.

"Sounds like your phone."

"Oh."

He got up to answer it while I picked mine up to send Aleks a text. When I put my cellphone down, I looked at Charlie, noticing his sudden change straight away. He turned around, looking worried.

"My parents are inviting us for dinner," he said and placed the phone against his chest.

"Would you like to go?"

"Yes, but…"

"Is everything okay?" I asked.

"Yeah, yeah, I um…do you want to come with me?"

I chuckled. "I would love to. Besides, your family already loves me," I said, hoping he'd feel reassured with whatever he was struggling with.

It seemed to work because he rolled his eyes and smiled, pulling the phone up to his ear to let them know we'd be there later.

Charlie tore the drawing from the sketchpad and gave it to me before he went back to his room to get ready.

I walked to the window with the drawing in my hand. I looked at it again in the brighter light now that it had stopped raining. I had no clue what to do. No surprises there.

Maybe I could speak to Aleks. She'd know what to do.

I stared at the view outside the window and saw

Tristan chatting to Olly, who was pointing at some flowers. My cellphone rang, making me jump.

"Hello?"

"Hey, Brat, how's it going?" Aleks's voice was like a soothing balm washing over me. I hadn't realized how much I'd miss my sister while I was away.

"How are you? How's Dad, is everything okay?"

"The king is fine. I know you told me you don't get good signal there, but I don't know, I just had this feeling…"

"I'm glad you called. I need advice."

"Of course."

"Aleks, I'm falling for someone, and I don't know what to do." I sat on the edge of the bed and rested my head on my hand.

"What happened?"

"I met this guy. He's staying in the apartment next to mine. He's really sweet and perfect, so talented, and I can't look in his eyes without wanting to tell him how I feel."

Aleks sighed on the other end of the line. "Does he feel the same way?"

"I don't know. I think so."

"But he doesn't know who you are."

"Yeah, and there's more. I'm meant to be his fake boyfriend at his sister's wedding."

Just saying it aloud made my stomach turn. Because it sounded ridiculous, and because I didn't want to be a fake anything. I wanted it to be real. I wanted to explore these growing feelings and see if Charlie felt the same way.

Aleks laughed.

"Aleks?"

"Oh my god, Brat. Are you serious?"

"Yes!"

"I can name off the top of my head at least five novels on my bookshelf with fake boyfriend stories, and one of them even has a prince."

"Yes, yes, very funny," I said, rolling my eyes. "Any tips on what I need to do for a happy ending?"

Aleks was silent for a moment. When she spoke, her voice was steady and firm.

"Real life isn't like a novel, Kris. If you really have feelings for this guy, you need to tell him the truth. If he accepts you for who you are, that's great, but he'll need to understand what comes with being in a relationship with a prince. Not many people would want this life."

"What do I do if he doesn't?"

"You'll need to let him go, Brat."

What Aleks said wasn't news, but after hearing it, I knew I'd need to tell Charlie, well, eventually. I wasn't quite ready to lose what we had, especially after today.

"Thanks, Sestra."

"You're welcome."

I got ready quickly and knocked on the connecting door before going into Charlie's apartment.

He looked good enough to eat in his tight jeans, white shirt, and navy suit vest on top.

"What do you think?" Charlie asked.

I dragged him to me and inhaled the scent of his aftershave. "Hmm, edible." I kissed the side of his neck and bit the lobe of his ear.

"We'll never make it to dinner at this rate," he said.

I kissed him one last time and let him go, albeit reluctantly.

"Let's go. We don't want to keep your family waiting."

"Says he who's started with the post-dinner activities already."

"Baby, you're the starter, main course, dessert, *and* post-dinner activities," I said in a deep husky voice I almost didn't recognize as my own. "No matter what I'll have for food, I can guarantee I'll still want to ravish you later if you'll let me."

"Fuck."

I didn't miss Charlie adjusting himself as we walked down the long corridor to the main stairs of the Old Mill. Tristan really was doing a great job with the look and feel of the building. I'd noticed how touches of color appeared in some areas, blending the industrial origins of the building with its new incarnation as a place for people to live in and socialize.

---

Charlie stopped a few feet short of his parents' front door.

"Hey," I said, turning him to face me and tilting his chin up so I could look into his eyes. "It's going to be fine. I've got you, okay?"

"Yeah, okay."

Hannah opened the door with a bowl of chips in her hands.

"Come in, guys. Dinner's nearly ready."

"Does Mom know you're ruining your appetite?" Charlie asked, picking a few chips himself.

"Nope, and you're not telling her either."

She turned toward the stairs, but Charlie stopped her and whispered, "Is Rory here?"

Hannah narrowed her eyes. "No, why would he?"

"Isn't he staying here while his apartment is having work done?"

She waved her hand. "That was all finished days ago. He's back at his place."

I would have been angry that Charlie had had to stay away from his family because of this guy, and he wasn't even here anymore, but seeing Charlie relax turned my focus where it should've been, him.

"Come on, sweetheart. You have some childhood photos to show me."

"What?" he said and blinked in shock.

"I believe it's in the boyfriend manual. Letting the parents embarrass you by showing all your baby photos."

"That is correct, darling," Charlie's mom said, appearing out of nowhere, hugging us both. "If you want to wait in the lounge, I'll call you when dinner is ready. We can do embarrassing photos after."

I followed Charlie farther into the house as he mumbled something about betrayal and family. I pulled him to me so his back was to my front and put my arm around his waist.

"You also get to show me your childhood bedroom," I whispered in his ear so no one else could hear. "Guess what the boyfriend manual says about that."

He let out a small groan and continued to lead us to the lounge where his dad was nursing a beer in front of the TV.

Martin invited us to grab a drink and watch a soccer game with him. I could tell Charlie wasn't sure what to do, so I sat on one of the sofas and pulled Charlie so he was snuggled against me. He relaxed a little, leaning into me, and lacing our fingers together.

We sat in silence for a while until the soccer game got exciting.

"Oh, come on, he was clearly offside," Martin shouted at the TV.

"I agree," I said. "The referee needs an eye test. It was clear the guy was in the wrong place."

We clinked our bottles together, and I noticed Charlie staring at me.

"You okay, baby?" I whispered.

He nodded and looked back at the TV.

Charlie's mom announced dinner just as the game finished and within seconds Hannah, Ellie, and a guy I assumed was Charlie's brother, Connor, joined us at the long wooden dining table in the kitchen.

"So, you're the guy I keep hearing about," Connor said, shaking my hand. "Nice to meet you, man."

"Nice to meet you too."

"Okay, who's going to tease Charlie about bringing a boyfriend home for the first time ever?" Hannah asked and five hands raised.

I chuckled as Charlie went beet red.

"Mom, Hannah had chips before dinner," Charlie said.

"Connor had cookies for lunch," Hannah said.

"Dad has a bag of Hershey's Kisses hidden in the garage," Connor said.

I looked around, waiting to see who was going to tell on Caroline, but they just looked at one another and all said in unison, "Mom never does anything wrong."

I could have cried at that moment, but I didn't have time to analyze my feelings before Caroline spoke.

"That's right, I don't. And you're fools if you think I don't know about your dad's kiss stash."

She passed around the various plates of food before leaning over to Martin for a kiss.

My chest felt so tight. I had to consciously put food in my mouth, smile, and talk in the right places so it didn't look like I was just staring at the family in front of me. Which I was, because it was clear they all loved one another. For each time they teased one another, there was a story about when they did something good. My favorite was when Connor taught Charlie to swim and then the first time Charlie swam in the river without any help.

I could have watched the scene forever, so when we finished dessert I almost felt loss for the ending of such a perfect family dinner.

That was until Charlie gave me a heated look and whispered, "Wanna see my room?"

## 16

## CHARLIE

To say I'd been nervous about this family dinner was an understatement. I had been dreading Rory being there, so it had been such a relief when Hannah told me he wasn't. I was also angry with him that his apartment was suddenly ready so shortly after his plans to share my room were turned upside down.

Had he lied about it and then backtracked when he'd realized I hadn't fallen for it?

When I'd stopped short of going inside the house I'd grown up in, Rory had been on my mind, but there was also something else that I hadn't wanted to admit to Kris. I had never brought a boyfriend home. Hell, my parents had never even met anyone I'd dated before.

Kris had already met them, so I wasn't worried

about that. He could totally charm the pants off anyone, and I was right at the front of that line. But bringing him home, however, felt different, like we were doing something we couldn't come back from.

Watching Kris participate in my family dinner was wonderful. If I hadn't known better, I'd have thought he'd been coming along for years. And that was something else that worried me. My family liked Kris, that much was clear. How would they react when they found out we weren't together anymore?

By the time we got to the dessert course, I was ready to find an excuse to bolt, but then Kris decided to share my mom's homemade ice cream and pie. For each spoonful he fed me, he also took one for himself. The bobbing of his Adam's apple as he swallowed had a direct effect on how tight my jeans felt, and it wasn't because I'd eaten too much at dinner.

When our eyes met, I tried to send him a murderous look, but instead, I was lost in his dark heated gaze. Remembering what he'd said earlier, I gathered a confidence I was sure had only grown since meeting Kris and invited him up to see my room.

Not jumping him as soon as we walked inside the room was an exercise in self-restraint. Instead, I stood aside as he explored my bedroom, looked at the photos on the wall, and especially the numerous drawings I'd made from when I was barely old enough to hold a pencil to those I'd drawn just before I'd moved out to go to college.

"You were adorable," he said, looking at a photo of me, Hannah, and Connor at the river. We stood in height order, Hannah and Connor with their light blonde hair on either side of me. Connor was holding up a fish he'd caught with our dad and Uncle John.

"Strawberry Shortcake."

"What?"

"That's what they called me. Strawberry Short-cake, because I was the only one with my dad's red hair. I used to hate it."

Kris sat beside me on the bed and ran his hands through my hair.

"I love your red hair," he said. "Come here."

He sat farther back on the bed and pulled me so I didn't have a choice but to straddle him. My arms went around his shoulders and my hands ran through his coal-black hair.

"Kiss me, Kris."

"You never need to ask," he said before our lips met in a frenzied kiss. He tasted of vanilla and apple, my second favorite flavor after pumpkin spice, although I wondered if every flavor from Kris's mouth would become a favorite.

His tongue massaged mine in a slow dance that made the rest of the world vanish.

"Charlie."

My name sounded like a prayer coming from his mouth as his lips left a trail of soft kisses all around my neck. I pressed harder against him when he untucked my shirt, and I felt his warm hands on my skin.

There was a new kind of desperation to do more than kiss and touch, and I knew it wasn't coming just from me.

Fortunately, or unfortunately, a knock on the door stopped us from taking things any further.

"Charlie, we're going over to the Falls. Are you guys coming?" Hannah said through the door.

I smiled into Kris's mouth. "She totally knows what we're up to here, or she'd have barged in."

Kris gave me one last kiss before he straightened my vest and shirt. "What is the Falls."

"It's a bar. Do you want to know where Chester Falls got its name?"

"If you're talking about real waterfalls, then I'm down for it. God knows I need cooling down," he said and fell back on the bed with a frustrated sigh.

"We'll be down in a minute," I shouted back at my sister.

It had been a few years since I'd last been at the Falls, but it hadn't changed one bit. It was a glorified log cabin with a bar and a bunch of high tables with stools and plenty of space for people to move and dance when they had live music bands playing.

Ben waved at us from the bar and pointed at where Tristan was sitting. Ellie went straight to Ben while the rest of us headed to the table Tristan was saving.

"Hey, guys, thanks for coming. Ben's been really nervous about his wedding speech, so I figured the distraction would be good," Tristan said and then looked at where Kris's hand rested on my waist.

"Kris, can I ask you a few questions about the apartments? Just want some general feedback." Tristan asked.

Kris whispered in my ear to not worry and then they left toward the terrace where it was considerably less noisy.

It was just Connor, Hannah, and me at the table, so, as usual, when our parents weren't around, they ganged up on me. I smiled at my foregone, but correct conclusion.

"So, little brother," Connor started, "how did you bag yourself that hunk of a man?"

"Since when do you appreciate men?"

"Come on, Charlie, I'm into girls and even I know he's hot," Hannah said.

I looked toward the bar to see if Ellie and Ben were any closer to coming back with drinks. I hadn't expected to be cornered by my brother and sister on my own, and so far, the topic of how I'd met Kris, surprisingly, hadn't come up.

"What do you want to know? Boy meets boy, they like each other, they date."

Hannah smiled and put her hand over mine. "Sorry, we didn't mean to pounce on you. It's just that we've never had a chance to meet one of your boyfriends, and now, here he is. Kris seems very nice, and I can tell he's totally smitten."

I raised my eyebrows. "Smitten? Excuse me while I go put on my britches and saddle my horse."

"Is that what kids are calling it these days?" Ben said, placing a few beer bottles on the table and looking all too pleased with his joke.

I grabbed two beers and stood up. "Is the cave still there?"

Connor winked at Hannah before nodding.

"You better not follow us, or else." My parting

words carried no weight because if there was a code of honor, we all followed it was that the cave was sacred.

I'd promised Kris I'd show him the falls, and considering my siblings' mood this evening, it was best I kept Kris away from them.

Kris and Tristan were on the way back, so I just grabbed his hand and pulled him back in the direction of the terrace.

I hoped the path to the falls hadn't changed in the years since I was last there because I didn't want to make a fool of myself by getting lost. Although considering present company, maybe it wouldn't be too bad.

"Where are we going?" Kris asked.

"Secret spot."

The path was more overgrown than I remembered, but it was still there. Using the flashlight on my cellphone, I led us down the steps from the terrace of the bar down toward the waterfall.

The noise of the cascading water became louder as we got closer. A few more yards and I saw the gate my brother had put up with the sign saying "private property."

"Are we going onto someone's property?" Kris asked.

"Nah, Connor put the gate here so people

wouldn't go farther and find this place."

I purposefully pointed the light at the ground when we entered the cave and then asked him to sit on the rock bench.

"Close your eyes," I said and then turned the lights on. "You can open them now."

I wasn't sure the lights would still work, but I'd guessed from Connor's smile earlier that this was a place he still came to hang out.

"Oh my god."

Kris's reaction as he saw the lights that reflected from the waterfall into the cave was everything. My throat felt so tight I couldn't speak, so I sat beside him on the rock.

"What is this place?" he asked after a few minutes.

"Chester Falls is named after these waterfalls. The fast flow of the water is the reason for the location of the Old Mill downstream and how the town started up some two hundred years ago."

"No, Charlie," he said, pressing closer to me and looking straight into my eyes, "what is *this* place."

"Oh, um, I found it with Connor when we were kids. At the time, there was this overgrown hedge a few yards into the path. We'd heard the water from the other side and decided to check it out. Eventually, we made it here and found the cave. It used to be our secret spot. At some point, we decided to bring some solar-powered lights so we could have parties here after dark, but when we saw the effect of the lights and the reflection of the water on the cave walls, we decided to keep it a secret."

Kris stared at me, but in the dim flickering lights, I couldn't see his eyes.

"Why did you bring me here?"

His voice was smooth like honey, different from the husky tone I'd heard earlier in my room.

"I...I don't know."

Liar. I was such a liar. I'd brought him here because I was selfish and wanted another memory with Kris. Sitting on his bed and drawing us was a memory he'd helped create, but this one was all mine, and I'd cherish it forever. Even after he was gone, after I was back in Boston, I'd hold on to it. The time when we became the couple I'd seen in the drawing all those years ago.

I was certain I'd never experience this feeling again, so I leaned farther into Kris and held on to his arms as they kept me warm.

"I think you brought me here to make out."

I shivered as his breath ghosted the back of my neck.

"That can be arranged," I said.

## 17

---

## KRIS

I FELT like a jackass for deflecting the moment and suggesting we make out. Not that I didn't want to make out with Charlie. In fact, I would gladly spend the rest of my life making out with him, and I'd die a happy man even if we didn't ever take things further.

Aleks's words were weighing on me, and if I already felt guilty for not telling Charlie who I was, now that he'd shared such an important thing with me, I felt worse.

The coolness of the rock seeped through my clothes and reached far deeper than skin level. Charlie straddled me the same way he'd done earlier and pressed his lips to mine.

"You know, making out requires participation from both parties, otherwise it's just creepy," he said.

I let out a small laugh I wasn't really feeling.

His body was warm against mine, so I pulled him closer, hiding my face between his neck and his shoulder blade.

"Is everything okay?" he asked, a tinge of worry in his voice.

I nodded. "Let me just hold you, okay?"

He didn't answer, but his fingers ran through my hair, soothing me with every pass.

"Thank you for sharing this place with me. It means so much more than you'll ever know," I said, my voice muffled against his skin.

Charlie laughed softly, which made me look up at him. I couldn't see the pink tone of his face, but I knew it would be there from the way he was biting his lip and avoiding my eye contact.

"The reasons for bringing you here are far more selfish than sharing my secret spot."

"Oh really?"

"Uh-huh."

Charlie got up from my lap and went into a part of the cave that was in the dark. He took his cell-phone out and looked for something in a box.

"Ha. Here it is."

"What are you looking for?"

"Matchsticks."

I didn't think I could be surprised by Charlie, but then again, he'd been surprising me since the moment he fell on me.

The cave lit up one candle at a time, showing it was much deeper than I originally thought. On one side, next to the stone wall on the ground, were dozens of blankets.

Charlie got up from tidying the blankets and turned to me. Each step in my direction was like a promise. Was this really happening?

"I changed my mind, Kris," Charlie said. His hands came up to my chest slowly. They were warm and there was no hint of insecurity in his touch.

"About what?"

"I want you. Fuck complications. Fuck long distance. We're here now. I want to finish what we started in my bedroom, what we couldn't do against the tree earlier."

"Are you sure?"

Charlie nodded. I ran my hands down his back and settled them on his perfect tight ass.

"I need you to say it, baby."

"Yes, Kris. I really, *really* want your big cock inside me, and I want you to fuck me so hard I won't even remember my name when it's all over." I had no idea where this dirty-mouthed, assertive version of Charlie was coming from, but it turned me right the fuck on.

"Fuck me, Charlie."

I expected Charlie to kiss me or at least undress me, but instead, he unbuttoned his vest and then his shirt, keeping his eyes on mine the whole time.

He moved on to his jeans, but I couldn't just watch. I needed to touch him. I pushed his shirt and vest off and then went down on my knees. There was already a wet patch on his boxer shorts. I wondered if it was from now or earlier.

"Touch me, Kris," he said with confidence.

My hands covered his hard cock that was hardly being restrained by his underwear. I pressed my face to it and inhaled his musky scent. Charlie gasped but then moaned when I licked the outline of his cock and pushed his underwear down only enough to get my lips around the head.

I sucked and licked until he started pushing farther inside my mouth. I let him go with a pop and pulled his jeans and underwear all the way down and off.

Charlie lay down on the blankets and opened his legs like he was offering himself to me. My clothes came off so fast I was pretty sure at least one of the buttons of my shirt popped.

"Jesus, Charlie, look at you." I traced his skin, watching as his muscles contracted in reaction to my touch, and little goose pimples followed the trail of my fingers.

The need to be inside him and feel him around my cock as he came undone was unlike anything I'd ever felt, especially as I normally bottomed.

Being in the cave in candlelight was like being in a magical place, something that only existed in fairy-tales. I almost laughed aloud. Here I was, a real-life prince, about to make love under the stars and candlelight to someone who looked at me with so much trust I felt like a king.

"Please, Kris."

I didn't want him to beg; he didn't need to because I was as desperate as he was. I sheathed my own aching cock with the condom and opened the packet of lube I took out from my wallet.

Charlie thread his slim fingers through my hair and pulled me down for a kiss. His little moaning sounds as I added one finger and then two nearly took me over the edge.

"Fuck, Charlie, you're going to feel so good around me."

"Then do it already. I want to come with you inside me."

When I moved up, Charlie wrapped his legs around me. His skin was so warm against mine. I pushed in, feeling the tight ring of muscles resisting against the head of my cock before he relaxed.

Nothing had prepared me for the tightness, heat, and excruciating pleasure of being inside Charlie. Drops of sweat ran down my back as I struggled to go slow.

"Please, Kris."

"Shh, I don't want to hurt you, baby," I said.

"You won't. Just fuck me already," he demanded.

"Who knew shy little Charlie would be so bossy in bed," I said, pulling out and pushing all the way in. He closed his eyes, but I could tell it wasn't from pain.

The skin between us was as hot as a furnace, which was a contrast to the cool air from the waterfall and humidity I felt on my back.

"So good, Kris. You fuck so good."

I was getting close, so I wrapped my hand around his cock and stroked him until he screamed his release. Before he came down from the high, I increased my pace, hitting his prostate over and over again and drawing out his orgasm as I filled the condom with my own.

Our harsh breaths mingled together in a kiss, both of us were reluctant to stop. Once I withdrew from Charlie and got rid of the condom, I pulled one of the blankets on top of us, hoping to prolong the feeling of rightness, happiness, and love that was currently running through every cell in my body.

The following minutes were filled with unrushed kisses, hands exploring warm skin, and giggles caused by not so warm feet.

"Hey, it's the first time we've ended up on the floor without you falling over me," I said.

"Nope, second time." Charlie leaned over and whispered in my ear, "The first time was—" I cut him off with my mouth on his.

Charlie's cellphone dinged, pulling us back to reality.

"That's Connor. They're getting a cab home."

"Maybe we should do the same."

We got dressed and made sure all the candles were out before we left the safety and fantasy world of the cave.

On the way back to the apartments, while Charlie nodded off against my chest, I texted James about the rehearsal dinner the next day.

"You look great," Charlie said when I crossed the threshold between the two apartments.

I shook my head. Charlie was the one who looked stunning in his suit and his red hair styled like it was messy but not quite.

When we got in the car, I gave James a nod to let him know everything was okay. We'd agreed James would park the car near the venue and sit in the bar, keeping an eye on anyone that might look like they recognized me, particularly that journalist, Ceecee Bloomfield. Once we were in the private room with the rest of the dinner guests, it wouldn't be too bad.

"I never asked you yesterday. How is your brother? He seemed okay at the dinner with your parents," I said.

"He's not well. I don't know if he's coming down with something or just tired. I guess it doesn't help that his girlfriend is the Wicked Witch of the West."

I looked at Charlie, who was staring out of the car window.

"She has a troupe of flying monkeys?"

Charlie looked back and smiled. "Sorry, that wasn't very kind. She's just not my favorite person."

I got as close Charlie as I could, considering the

seatbelts, and placed a kiss on his head. I didn't miss James's look in the rearview mirror but chose to ignore it.

"Maybe he'll talk when he's ready."

"Yeah, maybe."

"Are you looking forward to the dinner?"

Charlie lit up. "Like you wouldn't believe it. Ellie's parents are super nice, but it's her uncle you need to watch out for. He's a flirt and has spent the last three years trying to convince Uncle John and Aunt Gina that they need to be in a throuple."

"A what?"

"A three-way relationship."

"Is that a thing?" I'd never heard of it before.

Charlie chuckled.

"What's so funny?" I asked.

"You, believing what I just said."

I laughed and poked Charlie in his side, making him giggle.

"So, Ellie's uncle isn't interested in John and Gina?"

"Nope, but he is a flirt so watch out."

"You're not going to save me from the big bad wolf?"

Charlie laughed harder.

"I'll be running a mile. As it is, he's already asked me once if I wanted him to be my daddy."

I stopped and stared at Charlie, suddenly feeling jealous that another man might be hitting on him. That was until Charlie pulled me in for a quick kiss and said he was joking.

"You're in a good mood," I said.

"I am. I'm looking forward to the dinner, and you need to chill because you look like someone's about to come at you from behind and attack."

I smiled and put my arm around Charlie.

"I'm just a little nervous, I guess."

Having James around was reassuring, but it was still a risk being in public. Somehow, the thought hadn't even crossed my mind last night when I was at the Falls bar.

The events of the night before had been running in my head like a movie on playback ever since. Whether or not we called it fucking, there was no shadow of a doubt that I'd made love to Charlie. Had he known? Or did he see it as just fucking?

James couldn't come inside the hotel at the same time as us, so I was extra aware of my surroundings. Since we'd talked on the phone, I'd learned that Ceecee Bloomfield was a total shark who worked for a famous publication known for twisting headlines based on not much more than a blurry photo.

They were the same publication behind the first photo that had caused me to need to lay low, even though I wasn't the one in the photo, and I hadn't even been anywhere near the event.

At least it didn't seem that Ceecee was in any way connected to that particular article or that she had recognized me when we'd met at the bar. The lack of press presence in Chester Falls was a testament to that.

I took Charlie's hand in mine as we walked through the lobby of the hotel and followed the signs to the room where the dinner was being held.

"Charlie, my love," Charlie's mom said as soon as she saw us.

"Good evening, Caroline," I said as I took her hand, placing a soft kiss on it.

"Oh, Kris." She blushed the same pretty pink as Charlie. "You kids look so happy together. What a way to make a mom proud."

Charlie blushed at his mom's words.

"Please excuse me, I need to go to the men's

room," I said as I let go of Charlie's hand and tried my best to not run toward the restrooms I'd seen on the way in.

Luckily, there was no one else there, so I locked myself in a cubicle and let the tears flow.

## 18

## CHARLIE

"Mom, I'll meet you inside. I'm just going to check if Kris is okay," I said, kissing my mom's cheek.

"You go, my dear. Take your time. They're starting with speeches, so you don't need to worry about being there for that."

I hugged my mom. She was the best person ever, and I had a little moment of regret for not seeing her more. I needed to change things after the wedding, but now, my priority was Kris.

"Kris? Sweetheart, are you here?" I called.

"In here."

I saw the door of the disabled cubicle opening, so I went in. Kris was sitting on the floor with his back to the wall. He had his head down on his knees. I knelt next to him.

"What's up, sweetheart?" I asked, running my fingers gently through his hair.

He looked up and his eyes were red and his face was wet from crying. I touched Kris's knee so he'd straighten his legs. When he did, I straddled him, reached out for a piece of tissue, and put my hands on either side of his face, wiping the tears dry.

"Your mom. I'm sorry, Charlie, it was just... I haven't had a mom treating me like a son in such a long time, so even though I know it's not for real, it still got to me. I'm sorry."

"It's okay, come 'ere."

I pulled Kris into my chest, which was easy since I had a height advantage sitting on his legs. I held him for the longest time until he straightened up.

"What a head case, hey?" Kris joked.

"Ugh, even with a tear-streaked face, you're still the most beautiful man I've ever seen," I said, kissing him. "I hate you."

"No, you don't."

"No... I don't."

When we made it to the dinner, Ben, who was Ellie's best man slash man of honor, was doing his speech, so we hung by the door, waiting for it to be over so we could take our seats. Kris stood next to a pillar and pulled me in front of him, wrapping his arms around my shoulders.

"I've never been to an American wedding, but isn't this meant to happen at the wedding?" Kris asked.

"Yes, but Ellie and Hannah wanted the speeches only for close family and friends, and the wedding day to party."

I scanned the room to see who was there and saw where my family was. Ellie and Hannah were sitting as close together as was possible without actually being on each other's laps. I smiled to myself, and when Hannah made eye contact, we waved at each other.

She winked and then moved her head to the right. I followed the direction until my eyes fell on Connor and finally on the Wicked Witch.

She was staring at me with eyes wide open.

When I didn't move my gaze, she relented and turned to speak to Connor. I couldn't see Connor because his back was to me. I wondered how he was feeling today. I'd almost seen traces of my older brother during dinner and at the bar yesterday, but there was an underlying sadness in his eyes.

"Will this take any longer? I'm starving."

I chuckled. Kris was right, we hadn't really had lunch, so I was also fairly hungry.

"Hopefully not, or I might have to start nibbling on you," I said, taking Kris's hand from where it rested on my chest to suck and bite his thumb.

Kris drew in a breath, and I felt his erection against my back.

"And now we need the speech to go on a little longer, you fucking tease."

I turned my head and kissed Kris. God, we were so good together.

We were both glad when the speeches were finished and food was served. We'd ended up on the same table as Uncle John and Aunt Gina, which was a relief.

I'd noticed Rory at a table on the other side of the room. We didn't make eye contact, but Kris must have seen Rory, too, because all of a sudden, Kris's chair was moving closer to mine, and his arm was on the back of my chair.

"Look at you, all caveman-like," I whispered.

"Just marking my territory, baby. You're all mine."

"Oh really?"

"Yup, ever since you fell all over me in the hallway."

I looked at Kris with the most indignant look I could muster.

"Excuse me? I believe I was pulled down."

"Aw, look at you two," Aunt Gina said. "Charlie, darling, I'm so happy you found someone at last. I was starting to get worried."

"Me too," Uncle John said. "She was about to get the cast of the local *Magic Mike* to turn up at your doorstep one by one and offer to date you."

"Can that still happen?" Kris asked, wiggling his eyebrows up and down.

I stared at him until we both laughed.

"Aunt Gina, please do not send men to my apartment. You know Tom doesn't do well in the presence of other members of the same species."

"Have you met Tom?" Gina asked Kris. "He's Charlie's adorable roommate. Such a sweetheart."

I rolled my eyes.

"She only likes him because he's the only one who can cope with a whole day of shopping in Macy's with her."

"That and he has a knack for cocktails."

I nodded my agreement. They always came back from their shopping trips with more bags than they could carry, and Aunt Gina a little more on the drunk side than the tipsy one.

Kris rubbed his hand up and down my arm. "Um Tom, he…well, you know, are you…"

I put my mouth near Kris's ear and whispered, "Are you asking if Tom and I had adult nap time? Bumped uglies? Did the dirty deed?"

Kris coughed.

"No, sweetheart," I said, placing a hand on his thigh. "Tom and I are just friends." And then I kissed his cheek.

Kris put his hand on top of mine and squeezed. "I'm glad. He sounds like a fun person for your aunt, and I'd hate to have him killed."

I chuckled.

We made pleasant conversation with the rest of the guests at the table and enjoyed the good food. I glanced toward Hannah a few times. I couldn't believe in just two days my sister was going to be married to the love of her life, and I couldn't be happier for her. Ellie was a phenomenal person and like another sister.

I looked around for Connor and saw that he wasn't at his table. The witch, as usual, was on her cellphone, ignoring the other guests on her table.

"I'm going to look for Connor," I said to Kris when the main course flatware was cleared.

"I'll come with you."

We excused ourselves from the table and left the room.

"Where do you think he might be? The restrooms?" Kris asked.

"Either there or outside."

We started with the male restrooms but found them empty, so we went outside. Connor wasn't in the parking lot, either, so we looked around the building. Fortunately, it was still light enough outside.

I spotted Connor sitting on a picnic table. He had his back turned, so he didn't see us approach.

"Con," I called.

Connor turned around but didn't change how he sat hunched forward.

"Hey, Charlie. Hey, Kris."

"Con, you're not okay. Please talk to me or I'll need to use combat tactics."

When we were growing up, Connor and I used to fight just like any other siblings, and when we did, Hannah used to get in the middle and punch us both until we apologized to each other. We never dared to tell our parents about her, and we were also very embarrassed that we'd been bested by a girl.

"I've been told we need to get married."

"You're engaged?" I said a little too loud and felt Kris's hand slip into mine.

"No, no, but she wants to. She's been really pissy, saying she didn't want to get married after Hannah."

"Is the woman for real? I'm sorry, Connor, if you love her, you do what you need to do and I'll respect that and support you. But don't you see how she behaves with other people?"

"I think she's just stressed with her new job."

"Okay, then, so what's the problem?"

"Um, just other stuff," Connor said.

"Okay."

"Okay?"

"Connor, whatever it is that you're struggling with, you can always come to me, but I would never force you to talk about anything before you're ready. You know where I live." I smiled and then stepped forward to wrap my arms around my older brother.

"Thanks, Charlie."

"What are you going to do about the wedding?"

"I'm not ready. I think I need to—"

Before Connor had a chance to finish, I heard high heels on the path. Sure enough, I turned and Ceecee was strutting our way.

She looked stunning in her red dress and with her

hair made up into a bun. There was not a single thing out of place, maybe just her personality.

"Hi, Ceecee," I said.

As usual, she ignored me and went straight to Connor.

"Babe, they're serving dessert Do you want to come in? Are you feeling better?"

I could tell her concern was an act, but there was nothing I could do or say in that situation.

Ceecee seemed to finally notice there were more people around. Her smile went from fake to super fake and then predatory.

"Your Royal Highness, we meet again."

My first thought was that she was now being bitchy, but then I noticed her eyes were locked on Kris who had gone as white as a sheet.

"What are you talking about, Ceecee?" I asked.

"Oh, poor Charlie. Dating one of the richest men in the world, a prince no less, and you have no idea? Or maybe he didn't want you to know so he could have his way and then discard you like he did his ex-boyfriend, Sergei?"

I turned to Kris. "What is she talking about, Kris?"

Kris opened his mouth and then closed it again.

"Oh bless, you're so cute." Ceecee touched my cheek before I pulled away.

"What's this about, Ceecee?" Connor asked.

"Nothing much, babe. Just my passport to that promotion I've been working my perky little ass for in the last year. Ceecee Bloomfield, Editor-in-Chief of *Monza* magazine. Has quite a ring to it, doesn't it?"

She took Connor's hand and they left me and Kris on our own. Connor looked behind and shrugged like he had no clue what was going on. That made two of us.

# 19

## KRIS

I'D GONE to a whole different country to run from the eyes of the press, and I'd found myself face-to-face with it, and the wrong kind, nonetheless. So much for trying to hide who I was and keeping a low profile.

I almost couldn't look at Charlie because I knew I'd need to tell him everything now, and the look in Charlie's eyes told me the walls around Charlie's heart were already going up.

"What was she talking about, Kris?"

"Baby—"

Charlie put his hand up.

"Sorry, Charlie. I am what she said. My name is Kristof Ivan Maxim, and I'm the prince of Lydovia."

Charlie's hands went to his mouth, and his eyes filled with unshed tears.

"Your clothes, you said your assistant got them, and then you backtracked. I knew you were wealthy, but I thought maybe you didn't want to show off so you could be a regular person."

That was exactly what I'd wanted, and I'd succeeded until Ceecee-fucking-Bloomfield outed me.

"I thought you were trying to get away from the ex you mentioned, or work stress—you know, the stuff that regular people want to escape from," Charlie said.

"I'm not a regular person, Charlie. That's why I couldn't say anything."

"No, no you're not. But I am."

And with that, Charlie walked away.

I ran my hands through my hair and paced the length of the gardens. I needed to tell Charlie how I felt, but I was afraid of going back inside the party in case Ceecee was talking about me. The last thing I needed was for the rest of the guests to know who I was.

Too many scenarios were going through my head. Charlie upset. The press swamping the place. The headlines that would be printed. Had Ceecee taken any photos of Charlie with me?

"Kris." James came running. "We need to get you out of here and back to the apartment."

"How about Charlie?" If James was worried about the press, I didn't want Charlie exposed to it. God knew what Ceecee meant when she was talking about me being the passport to her promotion.

"I just saw him leave. Maybe he's getting a cab back too." James kept looking around in all directions. The sun had gone down, so the only light came from the tiny lamps that lit the path to where we stood.

"Come on, you can tell me what happened in the car."

I left reluctantly, but I knew James was right. I needed to get to the Old Mill before the press could track me. I just hoped Ceecee didn't know where Charlie and I were staying.

"I really messed up, James," I confessed.

"What I saw earlier wasn't just two guys having fun, Kris. Even through the rearview mirror, I saw how you looked at him."

"I've totally fallen for him." I sighed and rolled down the window to catch some fresh air. "He didn't know who I was until tonight. That woman, Ceecee." I wanted to strangle her. She had no right.

"Have you seen the news feeds?"

"No."

James took his phone from his pocket, unlocked it with his thumb, and passed it to me.

"Look at the *Monza* app."

I searched for the app and tapped the screen. At the top of the feed was the photo that had caused me to go into hiding. It showed Sergei in a club surrounded by guys, and there were lines of drugs on the table. There was also a semi-hidden figure that the press had wrongly assumed was me.

The photo wasn't new, but the headline and the report were:

"*The Prince and the Pauper*—was Prince Kristof really at the drug-fueled party weeks ago with his boyfriend Sergei Nowak, or was the reason for his absence from recent royal family engagements something altogether different? Prince Kristof has been seen in America, the Connecticut countryside nonetheless, in the company of a young American aspiring artist, name as of yet unknown. Has Prince Kristof already moved on from the break-up with his long-term boyfriend Sergei? See Sunday's special edition of *Monza* magazine where the results of outstanding investigative journalism by our own Ceecee Bloomfield will uncover the latest scandal in the Lydovian royal family."

"Fuck. Fuck. Fuck!" I shouted. "They know about Charlie. James, what do I do? He can't be involved in this mess. He's too good and innocent for it."

James's cellphone rang at that moment, the call coming through the speakers in the car.

"James Bennet."

"James, my dear, we have a problem."

I recognized the voice of Mary, James's housekeeper.

"What's the matter, Mary?"

"The press is camped outside. Looks like they think Tonya's visit the other day was a gimmick to hide the fact that Kris was in the area. One evening paper has a photo of Kris with a man. They're walking in the rain."

"Mary, this is Kris. In the photo, can you see the other man's face?"

"No. His face is covered up because you were embracing, but my guess is whoever took that photo took many more, and they're building up the interest to print tomorrow."

"Thank you, Mary," James said. "Can you do me a favor and call Tonya and ask her to meet me in our usual spot?"

"Will do, dear. You two be careful."

James ended the call. We were close to the Old

Mill, so before James dropped me off, he left me with orders to not leave the building without further instruction.

As soon as I was in the building, I ran up the stairs and knocked on Charlie's apartment door. The lights were off, but I hoped he was in. I knocked again. Nothing.

I went inside my apartment. The key to the connecting door was on top of the fireplace. Without thinking twice, I grabbed it and opened the door. I turned the light on, and my heart sank when I saw Charlie's made-up bed without him in it. At least all his clothes were still there so he'd need to come back for them.

My cellphone rang, so I ran back to my apartment, leaving the connecting door open.

"Hello?"

"Kris," Aleks said. "I have the press office with me on this call. I understand that a member of the American press found you and saw you with your guy and reported on it."

Aleks's voice was assertive, but I could tell she was shaken by the news. My big sister would usually be shouting and swearing by now, but I suspected her act was for the benefit of the royal family press officer, Mr. Peeters.

"Your Royal Highness," Mr. Peeters said. "I deeply regret what happened, and I assure you we will work hard to manage the situation. The American press are sensationalist, but the good news is that the majority of the public these days doesn't believe a word that is printed. Having said that, I understand there's someone else involved?"

"Yes, Mr. Peeters, a man by the name of Charlie Williams," I said.

"What is his relationship to you?"

"What does it matter?" I paced the length of the room frustrated that the apartments faced the back of the building so I wouldn't see any cars approaching.

"Your Highness, we can't afford any curveballs on this one. Excuse the sports pun, my son is into those American games and watches them all the time. Anyway, I need to know so I can help Mr. Williams."

"He's my fake boyfriend." I cringed at my words. I knew how they sounded when I said them aloud, and they were also not a reflection of how I felt toward Charlie.

"I beg your pardon?"

"I met Charlie a few days ago. He's here for his sister's wedding. His ex-boyfriend was trying to get to Charlie, so I suggested I pretend to be his boyfriend so he was left alone. And yes, Mr. Peeters, I know how that sounds."

"I'm not here to pass judgment, Your Highness, just to do my job."

"Carl," I said, feeling defeated by the whole situation, "Charlie isn't just my fake boyfriend. He's a good person who doesn't deserve to be dragged in the press like this, neither do his family. He's…"

"I understand, sir."

Carl Peeters was a competent press officer; he'd worked for the royal family for a long time. I trusted him implicitly, but I was also scared. Somehow, when the press had attacked Sergei just after I'd publicly come out as gay and in a relationship, I hadn't felt like this. Maybe it was because Sergei wasn't just big in size, he also had a big personality and could deal with anything on his own.

Two hours later, there was still no sign of Charlie, and I was still waiting for a call back from Carl. I'd decided to stay in Charlie's room so I'd know when he was back. It was invasive, especially considering what was happening, but I needed to see Charlie.

Tiredness was getting to me, and I felt myself drift in and out of sleep. Without Charlie or news from Carl, there was nothing I could do. I resigned myself to getting some sleep in Charlie's bed.

The sound of a key in the door woke me up. I sat up straight in Charlie's bed and rubbed my eyes.

Charlie froze when he saw me.

"Please leave my room," Charlie said in a cold voice.

"Charlie—"

"No." He put his hands up to stop me from getting closer.

I saw Charlie's eyes were red, probably from crying, his hair was messy, and his dress shirt was untucked. He was still the most beautiful man I'd ever laid eyes on.

"Please let me explain, Charlie. You need to know exactly what we're dealing with. You may not forgive me or want to have anything to do with me, but at least you need to be informed, for your safety and your family's."

Charlie nodded and closed the door behind him.

"I wanted to tell you the truth, Charlie, you have to believe me."

"It's a bit too late for that, isn't it?"

"It's not easy growing up in the public eye. Everything you do is reported. What I did at school, how good my grades were, how I coped when my mom died, when I came out. Nothing is out of bounds to the press. The press in Lydovia mostly like the royal family, and they absolutely love my sister." I smiled as I thought of Aleks. "You know, she'd get along great with Hannah."

The corners of Charlie's mouth lifted slightly. I felt like I'd won the biggest prize ever.

"Because of who I am, I've had to always be aware of everything, and that meant I never had much contact with people outside my immediate family. Even my boyfriend…ex-boyfriend was the son of my former nanny. He grew up in the palace, so he knew what it was like for us."

"I'm sorry." Charlie said, "That sounds really awful."

"It's okay, it's all I know." And if that wasn't the truth.

"Is that why you're here?" Charlie asked.

I nodded. "Some bad photos came out, so my sister advised me to come to America and hide away until I have to attend the president's ball in a few weeks. I never thought I'd run into the most interesting, kind, and beautiful man I'd ever met. Charlie, I lied out of need and habit, not out of choice."

"So, what happens now? I don't want this to ruin Hannah and Ellie's wedding."

Just then my cellphone rang.

"That'll be my press officer." I answered the call

and put it on speaker. I wanted no more secrets or lies between us.

"Your Highness, we have a solution."

"Go on."

"We advise that you continue your fake relationship. We are trying to get in touch with Sergei to get to the bottom of the other photo, but in the meantime, reports that you are in a relationship and in love are good for you."

I looked at Charlie who looked like the rug had been pulled from under his feet .

# 20

## CHARLIE

I THOUGHT I'd been kidnapped and sent to an alternate dimension. One where talking about real-life princes and press damage control was a thing. Except I wasn't in an alternate dimension. It had really happened. Kris really had told me he's a prince.

When I'd walked away from Kris earlier, I hadn't known where to go. I hadn't wanted to involve the family, especially as I didn't know what was happening. All I'd known was that Kris had lied to me, and it had taken Ceecee outing him for him to come clean.

I'd walked miles, trying to get my conflicting thoughts in order. I'd tried to think of all the things I'd done with Kris over the last few days, the time we'd spent together. Yesterday. Was it all a bit of fun for Kris? I'd remembered the lady on the bus a week ago showing me the headline in the newspaper.

Was that only a week ago? So much had happened since then, it felt like a different life long ago in the past.

They'd been talking about Kris and his lifestyle.

Was Kris a playboy prince who'd decided to have some fun with a commoner who didn't know any better? I didn't read any of the gossip magazines, so I would never have recognized him.

Had it been a game? When I'd fallen over Kris that first time, was all that flirting a ruse?

I didn't want to believe that—well, I didn't know what to believe any more.

I was so embarrassed. I'd started believing in our own made-up relationship and had been caught up in how Kris had made me feel. For the first time in my life, I'd felt really wanted by another man, my opinions had mattered, my jokes were funny, and I was visible.

It had been so easy to fall for Kris. How fucking stupid.

"Charlie?"

"What?"

"Carl is suggesting we carry on with the fake relationship," Kris said.

I looked at Kris, really looked, but I wasn't sure what I was seeing any more.

"Why?"

Kris stared at his cellphone for a moment.

"Carl, I will call you back soon. Please work on a contingency plan." He ended the call and then faced me.

"I want to say how sorry I am, but none of the words seem right enough to express it, Charlie. Carl is just doing his job, which is to safeguard the royal family from the press and any scandals that could damage our reputation."

I suddenly got it. Yes, Kris had lied by not telling me who he was, but it was our fake relationship that had caused all this to happen. If Kris hadn't been with me, he'd have been safe at the Old Mill, and no one would have known about him. Ceecee wouldn't have seen him.

"Oh god." I covered my mouth and walked back until I hit a wall and let myself slide down to the carpet. "This is all my fault."

Tears I'd thought had run out during my walk were back with a vengeance.

"Oh no, Charlie, no."

Kris knelt on the floor next to me and ran his hands through my hair. I choked, remembering that only hours ago the roles had been reversed, and I'd been the one comforting Kris.

"Charlie, this isn't your fault. The press never stops. It would only have been a matter of time until they found me."

His warm hand rested on the back of my neck before he used it to tilt my head up.

"You don't have to do anything you don't want to do. Carl will stop any photos being printed, and so far, those that are out don't identify you."

"What do you mean? What photos?"

Kris went over to the bed to grab his cellphone and showed me a news app.

I scanned through the news about the prince of Lydovia being in Connecticut and scrolled down to see more photos. There it was, a photo of the two of us embracing as we'd returned from our rainy walk just after…

"Do they have photos of us? I mean…when we were…you know…"

I felt like I was going to be sick. I didn't want to imagine what my family would go through, the gossip in town, their names being dragged down in the local papers.

"I don't think so. Usually when they have something like that, they lead with it. I suspect they're building up for a big reveal of who you are."

That didn't make me feel any better.

"How will it work?" Charlie asked.

"What do you mean?"

"Our fake relationship. How will it work? What will we have to do?"

The tension in Kris's body disappeared, but his eyes told a different story.

"You really don't have to do it, Charlie." He sat next to me. "I used to wish I was a normal person. I wanted to walk to school instead of being driven, and I wanted to bring my friends home to play with me and my sister."

"You don't wish that anymore?" I asked.

Kris let out a choked laugh. "It comes and goes. I've used my expensive education and my influence to support charities in Lydovia. I used to do it mostly anonymously because I cared about the people more than publicity stunts, but it always backfires because when the press doesn't have anything good to say about you, they make up something bad."

"Is that what happened with your ex? They made up a story?"

Kris nodded. "When I came to America, I was determined to come up with a plan so I could continue to support the charities and do my work but be more visible with it to satisfy the press."

"And then I fell on you," I said with a smile.

"I had only arrived that afternoon. When you looked at me with those big green eyes, I panicked until I realized you didn't know who I was. With your cute flirting and your easy-to-be-around nature, you…" Kris paused, and I looked at him. "This is the first time in all of my life that I really wish I wasn't who I am. Even when my mom died and I wanted to be left alone to grieve, even then when I wished to just be a regular person, I didn't want it this bad."

I picked up Kris's cellphone from where he'd placed it on the floor next to us and handed it back.

"I need to understand what it is I need to do, and I want to make sure this doesn't affect my family or ruin Hannah and Ellie's wedding. Call your press person."

Kris turned to me and stroked my cheek. The damned butterflies in my stomach woke up. Maybe I was hungry.

"Thank you," Kris said, and I nodded back.

"One condition."

"Anything."

"I can't lie to my family. We need to tell them the

truth. Maybe not all of them, but certainly my parents, aunt and uncle, and my brother and sister."

"I wouldn't have it any other way, Charlie. Believe it or not, I didn't want any of this to happen, and I do care for your family."

"I know."

Kris called Carl, and together they came up with the plan that once we told my family the truth, we were going to record a short statement introducing me and asking for privacy.

I got up to use the bathroom. I was exhausted from the evening, the long walk to the apartment, and all of the feelings I was trying to keep hidden.

I'd left my sweatpants and T-shirt in the bathroom earlier, so I got undressed and got in the shower. Maybe once I felt clean on the outside, I'd also feel better on the inside.

Last night, I'd been ready to talk to Kris about our relationship. Now everything had changed, and I had no idea what to do with it all. My head started throbbing.

It was all too complicated. In what world would someone like me be in a real relationship with a prince? What would I even have to offer? That was assuming Kris even wanted to pursue a relationship with me, but then again, we were about to announce to the world we were together. How difficult would it be to go from fake boyfriends to real ones?

How would I go back to my job at Clarence's after this? Would the press follow me? What would they say about me being a store manager? My insecurities came flooding back. What had I just agreed to?

Kris wasn't around when I came out of the shower, but the connecting door to his room was open, and I could hear the shower. I went to my bed and lay down on top of the covers, closing my eyes, and hoping the headache would go away.

---

When I woke up, the sun was coming through the window, flooding the room with light. I looked at my cellphone and saw it was getting close to midday. At least I'd had a few hours' sleep, and my headache was gone.

I sat on the bed, and that's when I noticed Kris was asleep on the floor right next to my bed. It looked like he'd brought his pillow and comforter from his room too. I let out a long sigh.

I got out of bed as quietly as I could so I wouldn't disturb Kris, grabbed my cellphone, and went into

Kris's apartment, closing the connecting door behind me.

There was only one person I could trust to talk this through with.

"Hey, honeybun." I smiled at Tom's endearment and usual cheery voice.

"Tom, have you ever been in love?"

I could have heard a pin drop on the other end of the line.

"Tom?"

"Oh, honey." Tom's voice was laced with pity.

"What?"

"You know he's not worth it, right? I mean, I don't know him but from what you've said—"

"What are you talking about?" I was confused. Tom didn't know Kris, or at least I hoped the news hadn't spread and revealed who Kris's "new boyfriend" was.

"Rory, honey, you can't get back with him."

I laughed because Rory was the absolute last thing on my mind. In fact, it looked like Rory had been trying his best to avoid being in the same location as me, so much so I hadn't bumped into him at all the night before.

"Tinker Bell, I'm not talking about Rory."

"Oh. My. God. Tell me everything."

So, I did. Well, I spared some of the details, but I shared the rest with Tom. I knew Tom would never tell our story to anyone.

"I am fabulous," Tom sang.

"I tell you I am in love with the prince of a small European country and that the press might be knocking on my door any time and *that's* what you have to say?" I honestly wanted to laugh because Tom was so very…well, Tom.

"Yes. You can thank me by making me a knight or a sir or something when you're king consort."

"Tom, what on earth are you talking about?"

"I picked your fabulous wardrobe, you meet prince, prince falls all over your expertly matched clothes, and you live happily ever after."

This time I did chuckle.

"Can we get back to the real issue here?"

Tom sighed, and I heard him turn the coffee machine on.

"To be honest, I don't see a problem, Charlie. If you like each other and everyone thinks you're already in a relationship, why not try it out and see what happens?"

Tom made it seem so easy.

"I literally have nothing to offer him."

"What are you talking about? You have everything

to offer. You're my best friend, and you know how I'm picky with what I wear, so on that alone you should know I wouldn't just have any old best friend."

"Oh, Tom." I choked.

"Seriously, Charlie. I don't know the guy other than what I've seen in the magazines. If you fell for him, then he has to be a good person, too, because I know you. You wouldn't give your heart to just anyone. Trust that and let the rest fall into place."

"Thank you, Tinker Bell."

"You're welcome, honeybun."

Kris hadn't stirred next door, so I stepped out to the diner across the square and picked up coffee and pancakes for brunch. There was a lot to talk through today, and I couldn't do it on an empty stomach.

## 21

### KRIS

It didn't immediately occur to me the reason why my back hurt so much when I woke up until I heard Charlie's soft voice telling me to open my eyes.

"Hi," Charlie said softly. He was running his hands down my arm.

I sat up and leaned against the bed, bunching the comforter to cover my morning wood. I'd been dreaming about Charlie. It had been a nice dream, hence the hardness in the tracksuit pants I'd worn to sleep, but now I couldn't do anything about it.

"Morning."

"I went over to the diner and got us some breakfast."

"Thanks."

We stared at each other for a minute. I didn't dare

say anything for fear of breaking the spell. My hands were itching to touch Charlie, to tell him once again that I was sorry and that my feelings for him were more real than anything I'd felt my whole life.

Charlie broke the gaze first.

"Um, maybe you should get dressed."

"Yeah, sure."

I grabbed my stuff and went into my apartment. I was placing the comforter back on the bed when I caught sight of Charlie's drawing, which I'd put on the mantelpiece. I hovered my hand over Charlie's face on the drawing, tracing the outline of his cheek, his lips. It was time to face reality.

By the time we'd finished eating, Carl had already called twice with the arrangements for the rest of the day. It looked like the papers were still recycling yesterday's news, which gave us some time.

"I think they're waiting for us to either be silent about the reports or deny that they're true so they can print your real identity and run with it," I told Charlie.

"Okay, so we're meeting my family at my parents' and then we're recording a statement for the press, right?" Charlie asked. He looked unsure.

"Are you sure you want to go ahead with this?"

"Yes, um, I just don't know how to act with the

press... I mean, I've never met anyone famous or royal before. I don't know if I'm not allowed to look at you in public or touch you." Charlie blushed. "What if I do everything wrong and make you look bad?"

I wanted to hug Charlie something fierce. This was the kind Charlie I'd fallen for. Even though he'd been thrown in this situation, he was still thinking about me. I really didn't deserve him.

"Just act like you did before. I'm still me, warts and all."

Charlie sighed. "This would be so much easier if you did have warts."

I laughed.

"Right, are you ready for this? James should be waiting for us downstairs."

"James?"

"Oh yeah, um, the taxi we took yesterday? Wasn't a taxi. The driver, James, is my protection detail here."

"But I haven't seen him around."

"When I first arrived in America, the press found out I was staying with him, so they camped outside his property. He's been trying to distract them so they don't know I'm here."

Charlie nodded and got up to leave.

Just like the day before, I met James's eyes in the rearview mirror and nodded to let him know everything was okay.

James didn't leave our side as we walked into Charlie's family home. Charlie had called his parents and asked them to get the immediate family all gathered at theirs.

It wasn't totally unexpected that Charlie's mom virtually attacked us both with a warm hug. She was visibly worried, and considering Charlie hadn't given them any details, I wasn't surprised by her reaction.

"Hi, Mom," Charlie said.

I looked around the room and saw all the faces that were now familiar to me, but I did notice Ceecee wasn't there.

She'd mercilessly outed me to Charlie, but her magazine hadn't printed his name. It was hard to know what her angle was or what she was getting out of all of this, other than her prized promotion.

We took a seat on one of the sofas while some of the family sat on the other sofa. Hannah and Ellie, as usual, sat on the floor, and Charlie's dad and uncle were standing by the window. I took a deep breath to find my words.

All eyes were on me. I saw curiosity, kindness, and acceptance. Charlie's family, despite the lack of royal status, were just like mine. Or maybe it was the other way around, that my family, despite the royal status, still managed to be somewhat normal. There were things we disagreed on, but we were always there for one another. My mother's legacy.

Charlie interlaced his hand with mine. I hadn't even realized that at some point I'd looked down and closed my eyes.

"What's the matter, boys?" Charlie's dad asked. "Are you in some kind of trouble?"

"Caroline, Martin, Gina, John, Hannah, Ellie, and Connor, there's a reason we asked you to get together today," I said. "There is something you need to know about me and Charlie, but first, let me introduce you to Captain James Bennet."

It seemed no one had noticed James had walked into the room behind us. Everybody waved at James, and he simply nodded, although I didn't miss the tips of James's ears go a little pink when he set eyes on Connor, who'd narrowed his own. Any other time I'd have teased my friend about his attraction to Charlie's straight brother.

"James is my protection detail while I'm in America."

I let that sit and waited for the questions. Once again, I noticed Connor's reaction to my words and wondered if maybe he knew James. It was possible, after all, James had grown up in the area.

"Why do you need protection?" Charlie's mom asked.

"What do you mean while you're in America?" Hannah asked.

"When we met, I was introduced to you simply as Kris. The reality is that my name is Kristof Ivan Maxim, and I am the prince of Lydovia."

Charlie's hand tightened around mine as we heard the collective gasp. I looked at Charlie. This was the hard part now. Telling the family our relationship wasn't real. I didn't want to do it because in my heart, I'd be lying. To me, our relationship was the most real thing that had ever happened to me.

"Don't," Charlie whispered. He shook his head the tiniest bit, but I got it. Charlie didn't want me to tell his family our relationship wasn't real. I didn't know why. Maybe it was because he was embarrassed to say this had all started because he didn't want to turn up at the wedding on his own. I chose to believe that deep down, Charlie's feelings matched mine, and maybe, just maybe, there was a sliver of hope.

"Yeah," I said, turning back to the family. "I am so grateful and honored that you accepted me into the family, but I'm afraid I come with a caveat. The press got hold of photos of Charlie and me together on a walk the other day."

"That was you?" Ellie shrieked. "See, babe? I told you he looked familiar," she said to Hannah.

"My press officer is working hard to make sure no more photos are published. At this stage, Charlie's identity isn't known, but…" I looked at Connor who had his eyes down on the floor.

"My dear, no one in the family would tell on you," Charlie's mom said.

Charlie looked at me and then Connor. "Mom, Ceecee knows."

I couldn't read Connor's expression as he got up to leave the room. He apologized and walked to the door. James stepped in front of Connor and crossed his arms to stop him from going out. They were equal in size, so if their staring match escalated, there would be some damage.

"James," I called, "let him go."

"Kris, you don't know—" I raised my hand. Connor was Charlie's brother, so while I didn't know him well, I trusted Charlie, and so far, apart from Ceecee, I had no reason to distrust the family.

Maybe it was a testament to how stupid I was or to how stupidly I'd fallen for Charlie. At the moment, it was a toss-up between the two.

James let Connor pass, but not without first giving him a warning look.

"Son," Charlie's father spoke, "are you sure this is what you want? I can see you two care for each other, but a relationship with someone famous isn't easy, for either of you."

"Yes, Dad. I want to be with Kris, whatever it takes."

Martin nodded. "Kris, can you look after my son and make sure he's safe? And I don't just mean from the press."

I got the silent message. Charlie's dad was asking me if I could look after Charlie's heart.

"Martin, I won't let any harm come to Charlie," I said to Martin and then looked at Charlie, "from the press or otherwise. And that extends to all of you."

Charlie smiled. It was a warm, affectionate smile, almost intimate, like he was communicating something only we could understand.

"So, what happens now?" Ellie asked.

"We're going to intercept the press's plans by releasing a short video introducing me as Kris's boyfriend," Charlie said.

"I have my press officer working on this to make sure we can control the information that goes out. The public will be interested in Charlie, and I can't say I blame them," I said, putting my arm around Charlie, all my tension dissipating when he leaned into me.

"You might wonder how this will affect you once Charlie's identity is known. James is working with some friends he knows in personal security. We can arrange to have your homes secured as well as someone to accompany you wherever you go."

"Like bodyguards?" Gina asked. This time there were no jokes or flirtatious innuendos from Charlie's bubbly aunt.

"Yes. Neither you nor anyone else would know they're there, but if you needed assistance, they'd be there for you."

A knock on the door startled me.

"We're not waiting for anyone unless it's Connor coming back," Hannah said.

James opened the door and in walked Connor and Ceecee.

I noticed James's murderous look toward Connor's girlfriend, but my main concern was Charlie, who'd gone stiff beside me.

"Are you okay?"

"What is she doing here?" he asked.

"Charlie, Kris," Connor said, "we need to speak to you in private."

"Come on, people. Who wants a peak of the wedding dress?" Hannah said in a bossy voice. I caught her eye and smiled. She really was so much like Aleks.

"I'm going to check in with the wedding planner at the hotel," Ellie said, giving Hannah a kiss as she walked out of the main door, supposedly so she wouldn't see the dress herself.

As soon as everyone was upstairs, Connor and Ceecee sat on the sofa opposite. Connor kept looking at James.

"I'm sorry, Connor, he has to stay," I said.

Ceecee didn't look as made up as she had the night before. In fact, she was wearing a cotton dress and tennis shoes. It was like she was a different person, she almost looked pretty in a natural kind of way.

"I'm sorry," she said.

No one spoke or acknowledged her apology. She stiffened and took a breath.

"I've been under a lot of pressure at work to bring a new story in. I've been following the scandal with the Lydovian royal family, so when I saw Prince Kristof, I figured this was my opportunity to have the scoop on it."

"Do you really know what you've done, Ceecee?"

Charlie almost shouted and she flinched. "Just because someone has a title or is famous doesn't give you the right to intrude in their lives. How would you like to have a strange person photograph an intimate moment between you and Connor and then go splash it all over the papers?"

Charlie got up and walked to the window. His fists were clenched, and his face was red. I followed and wrapped my arms around him. Charlie hugged me back, relaxing slightly.

"Shhh, that's okay, baby."

"No, it's not okay." He turned to Ceecee. "Why do you always ignore me when you walk past?"

Ceecee looked uncomfortable. Connor just looked puzzled.

"I don't ignore you," she said.

Charlie stared at her, almost daring her.

"Okay, fine. I'm somewhat jealous of you, of your family, and how close you all are." Tears started running down her face, and I thought Connor would comfort her, but he didn't move an inch. It was like he was seeing his girlfriend in a new light.

"Why?" Connor asked.

"It's always been me and my mom. She raised me to fight for a better life. When you come from the poor housing developments, people look down at you. My mom always told me I was better than that life, that I deserved more."

"And it doesn't matter to you who you hurt along the way?" Connor asked.

Ceecee had the decency to look embarrassed. "I'm sorry. I didn't mean any harm. I was under so much pressure at work, so when I saw the opportunity, I jumped on it. I didn't think."

Charlie's eyes softened slightly, and I could see he was trying to empathize with her. Another reason as to why I needed to figure out a way to keep him.

## 22

## CHARLIE

"Ceecee, is there any way to stop the article you have coming out?" Charlie asked.

I was trying hard to not jump down her throat; unfortunately, her story did make me feel somewhat sorry for her. Not entirely, though.

"I don't know. My editor was quite excited about this, so I can't see how I could stop her now."

I looked at Kris, knowing we'd need to do the live press statement before Ceecee's article came out.

"I'll quit my job," Ceecee blurted. We all looked at her. "I know you won't believe me, but I am sorry."

She got up and left. Connor stayed where he was, his elbows on his knees, and his head resting on his hands. I wasn't sure if he looked deflated or relieved. James was staring at Connor with furrowed brows, looking like he wanted to do something but unsure of what.

"Right," I said, straightening my back. "Shall we get this show on the road?"

"You are amazing, you know that?" Kris said.

I wasn't sure what he meant. I was scared shitless of what we were about to do and what would come next. Most of all, I was scared I wouldn't have the courage to tell Kris how I felt, and that we'd part ways, and I'd never see him again.

Kris came forward and pulled me into a kiss. He kept it tame, but I felt it all the way down to my core. When I opened my eyes, Kris was looking at me like he was staring right into my soul.

"Charlie, I..." Kris didn't finish what he was about to say because at that moment, there was a knock on the door. Connor went to open it, and a second later, Rory came in followed by a giant of a guy I'd never seen before.

"I found this jackass in the hotel reception area being rude to people and asking for a Prince Kristof of Lydovia," Rory said, the last part in a deep voice as though he was imitating the other man, who still hadn't said a word. "Anyway, Ellie was walking past with the wedding planner and told me to bring him here. What's going on?"

My heart sank when Kris uttered one word, "Sergei," before he met the man halfway across the room and hugged him.

"Holy fuck," Rory said. "Charlie, is this true? Is he a prince?"

I found myself again in an alternate universe. My head started hurting. How had I found myself in a room with my ex-boyfriend, who was my brother's best friend and in the closet, my fake boyfriend who I wasn't sure was so fake anymore, my fake boyfriend's ex-boyfriend, my brother, who may have just been dumped by the maybe not-so-wicked Witch, and my fake boyfriend's security guard who seemed to have not got the memo that my brother was straight.

I needed to get some fresh air.

Kris caught up with me in the yard, and we walked in silence to the far end where a grouping of small trees offered some privacy.

"I'm sorry, it was getting too crowded in there," I said.

"Yeah, it was. I'm sorry. I've been trying to get hold of Sergei for ages, but I didn't realize he'd be coming to meet me. I thought he'd just call. Maybe Mimi did give him a good kick in the ass."

I laughed.

"What?"

"You said ass. Can princes say ass?"

"I must have missed that class. But it would be a shame," Kris said, coming closer with a heated look, "because I really do love ass. Yours in particular."

I did a twirl in front of him, jiggling my ass on purpose. Kris caught me as I turned back around, and I put my arms around Kris's neck, and we smiled at each other.

"We're not pretending anymore, are we?" I asked.

Kris shook his head. "I never was, Charlie. I never was."

Our lips met softly at first, almost like we were kissing for the first time. Kris's hands ran down my back, making me shiver under the touch, but it was when he touched my cheek after our kiss had ended that the final brick that was protecting my heart was obliterated to dust.

"I have totally fallen for you, Prince Kristof Ivan Maxim, or is it the other way around, of Lydovia," I said into Kris's eyes. "I don't know what the hell a prince would want with someone like me, but I really hope you—"

Kris stopped me with a kiss and then whispered against my lips, "I feel the same, Charlie Williams. I think I fell for you at the same time you fell on me."

"I'll never live it down, will I?"

Kris laughed. "I hope you keep falling on me and for me for the rest of our lives."

I knew this was only the beginning because, as far as the press was concerned, nothing had changed. Prince Kristof was still gallivanting with his new love interest in the American countryside.

"Come, baby. We'd better get back before the room gets trashed," Kris said. "There's too much unresolved sexual tension in there, and I think your parents won't appreciate the amount of testosterone currently in the air."

I laughed and took Kris's hand and followed him back inside. All the cars in the driveway were gone, so at some point, the family had left us. God, I loved them.

We opened the door to witness the strangest standoff.

James and Sergei were staring at each other like they wanted to cut each other's heads off. Connor was standing in front of James, seemingly trying to stop any fighting from happening. He was struggling to keep James back because despite looking as strong as each other, James was a trained army officer. Poor

Rory was trying to keep Sergei back and failing miserably. In fact, it looked like Sergei was trying to protect Rory from being the victim of a potential punch.

Kris and I exchanged a look. We were going to need reinforcements if the guys didn't back down.

The one useless talent I had came in handy in that moment. I put my hands to my mouth and whistled so loud everybody jumped back.

"You have superpowers," Kris said in my ear. "You have no idea how hot for you I am right now."

"Kris. Focus."

"Uh-huh."

I rolled my eyes at Kris.

"Sit down," I ordered, and within seconds, the two sofas were occupied. James and Connor on one, and Sergei and Rory on the other. I didn't miss how uncomfortable Connor and Rory looked, so I said they didn't have to stay. They both jumped at the chance to leave the room.

"Right. I believe we have some shit to work through," I said. Kris had an amused grin as he crossed his arms and watched me taking charge of the situation.

"Sergei, I'm Kris's boyfriend, Charlie." I extended my hand. Sergei took it but looked at Kris rather than at me.

"What are you doing here, Sergei?" Kris asked.

"The press has been hounding me nonstop since those photos were leaked. Someone named Ceecee Bloomfield got hold of my email somehow and said you were here and that you were with another man."

"Okay, one story at a time," Kris said. "How the hell did you let yourself be photographed with a bunch of rent boys and drugs?"

Kris sounded like he was struggling to contain his anger with Sergei.

"It was a setup. After you broke up with me, I went to stay with a friend. He said we should go to this party with his friend and chill. I didn't know what kind of party it was."

"Surely the drugs would give it away?" Kris said, deadpan.

"There were no drugs that I remember. I think my drink was laced with something because all I remember was that I wasn't having any fun, and all I could think about was you. The next thing I remember we were both back at my friend's house the next day feeling like death warmed up. Then those photos came out."

"Why didn't you say something?"

"I was embarrassed that I'd brought so much

shame to your family and my mom. I thought it would go away."

"Oh, Sergei." Kris sighed.

I felt sorry for the man. Loving Kris was so easy, and if nothing else, I sympathized with Sergei's feelings because I also didn't want to think of a future without Kris.

"I have an idea," I said. "How about we offer Ceecee the scoop on this. If she hasn't left yet, we can have her interview you and write the piece as we want her to. After all, she owes us that much."

Kris and Sergei agreed, so we called Connor back to the living room and asked him to call Ceecee. For a few hot minutes, I didn't think she was going to pick up the phone, but when she did, I took the cellphone from my brother and spoke to her myself.

Initially, Ceecee didn't want to do it, but I convinced her by accepting her apology and encouraging her to use the boost to find another job for a different publication.

Since she was basically scooping herself, her editor-in-chief agreed to stop the publication of the other article and replaced it with the interview, especially as they included photos of the happy couple too.

Carl was also on board and agreed it was a good way to wrap everything up.

The most important thing was that the press still didn't know Kris's exact location, so even if they swarmed the area after the interview came out, it wouldn't mess up Hannah and Ellie's wedding.

"You're smart and beautiful," Kris said into my lips as soon as we got back to the apartments later in the afternoon. Sergei was going to stay with James, and they'd promised they wouldn't kill each other. I'd asked why they hated each other so much, to which Kris had replied that they didn't, they were good friends, but when it came to protecting his friends and family, James was like a bull in a china store.

"I think you're the smart one," I said, pulling Kris's shirt out of his slacks and reaching for the warm skin and taut muscles of his back.

"Why's that?"

"You picked me."

Kris lifted me up and carried me to his bed. "I did pick you."

We laughed.

"Now, why don't we get rid of these stupid clothes," I said.

"See? Smart."

The last time we'd been together, it had been

quick, dirty, and slightly dangerous considering what I now knew, but this time we had all night and a soft bed.

"God, Charlie, you have no idea how much I've wanted to touch you like this again," Kris said as he removed my shirt and ran his hands over my chest.

His hands were warm, and his touch was soft, almost reverent. I didn't want that. Slow, yes, soft? Fuck no. I wanted hard. I wanted to feel everything Kris had to give.

"Stop treating me like a doll and remove my pants already," I demanded.

"Oh, I love bossy Charlie," Kris said, pressing his palm on my erection over my pants, eliciting a frustrated moan. "I fucking loved when you took charge earlier."

He undid the button and pulled the zipper down too slowly.

"I'll take charge again if you don't get to it."

Kris's smile made me shiver with anticipation. When he took my cock in his mouth and sucked all the way down to my trimmed hairs, I nearly saw stars.

"Fuck, oh fuck, Kris."

"I love it when you call my name, baby. Will you still call my name when I'm buried deep inside you?"

Kris said as he trailed kisses up my chest until he was feasting on my mouth.

"Why don't you grab a condom and find out?"

I missed Kris's mouth as soon as he stopped kissing me.

Kris jumped out of bed and removed his clothes quickly. I did the same, taking off my pants all the way as well as my underwear so I was fully naked.

I stroked myself, putting on a show for Kris, who tripped over his own feet in the rush to get back to bed.

"Shit," Kris said. "I don't have any condoms."

# 23

## KRIS

WHAT A TIME TO realize I hadn't brought any condoms with me. Fuck. As it was, I'd been lucky to have the one in my wallet the other day.

"My toiletry bag. My bathroom," Charlie said.

It took me a moment to hear what Charlie had said because the sight of him stroking his cock slowly enough to just take the edge off was keeping all of my blood flowing south of my chest.

When it did sink in, I ran to Charlie's bathroom, but not before stubbing my little toe on one of the legs of Charlie's bed.

"Shit. Fuck. Fuck." I hobbled over to the bathroom, my toe throbbing.

"You okay in there?" Charlie called from the other room.

I took a couple of condoms and the small bottle of lube from the bag and ran back to Charlie, this time avoiding another collision with any kind of furniture.

"Were you hoping to get lucky?" I asked as I resumed my exploration of Charlie's lush white skin.

"Uh-huh. I run into princes all the time; don't you know? Gotta be prepared."

"Oh really?" I loved this sassy, confident version of Charlie. Who was I kidding? I loved all versions of Charlie, and I couldn't be happier that we were together now, and I'd be able to get to know all of Charlie.

The Charlie under me now was sexy, demanding, and very much in need of relief, so I suited up and made sure he was carefully prepared to take in my length.

"Are you ready, baby?"

"Yes, fuck, yes please," Charlie begged.

I had intended on starting slow, but my body took over my mind when I was finally inside Charlie. It felt too good, too right.

Every move in and out of Charlie was hell and heaven combined. I flittered between the two until I felt the familiar point of no return. I wrapped my hand around Charlie's cock and stroked in synchrony with his own moves.

"Kris, oh yes…like that. Oh fuck, I'm gonna—"

I swallowed Charlie's cries with my mouth, and as we came almost at the same time, I couldn't think of a single thing other than Charlie. Charlie was everything.

When we were both drunk on love and lying in bed with limbs wrapped around each other, I smiled to myself. How naive to think not having sex would stop us from falling for each other.

"Things are going to get tough, Charlie," I said, needing to bring us back to reality and hating myself because I had to, "but I'm going to be with you every step of the way, okay?"

"Okay," Charlie said, clearly struggling to stay awake.

"Charlie?"

"Hmm?"

I smiled against Charlie's hair. I'd wait and ask tomorrow.

"Sleep, baby."

I couldn't remember a night when I'd slept so soundly as I did when I had Charlie in my arms using me as his own personal pillow.

How would it be when we had to be away from each other? I couldn't bear to think of it, but I knew it would happen. I couldn't just uproot Charlie to Lydovia. He had a family, a job, a roommate, and a life that, until this week, didn't include me.

Charlie stirred in my arms like a real-life déjà vu from a few nights before, except this time, I was free to touch him in any way I wanted, and to wake him up with sweet kisses.

"Hmm, I vote for waking up like this every day for the rest of my life," Charlie said as I trailed a path of open kisses all the way down Charlie's chest.

"I'll hold you to that."

I came back up to meet Charlie's eager mouth.

"You tease," he said, bucking his hips against mine to show me exactly how far south I should have gone.

"I wanted to ask you a question last night," I said.

"What question? I'm sorry, did I fall asleep on you?"

"No, I chickened out and let you fall asleep."

"I blame you for wearing me out," Charlie teased. "So, what was this question?"

I'd brought up the topic, but I still felt put on the spot.

"I wanted to ask if you'd ever consider living with me in Lydovia."

Charlie sat up, narrowly missing head-butting me and sending me over the other side of the bed and onto the floor.

"What?"

My heart sank. I knew it was a stretch; after all, we'd just met. Our relationship was unexpected, but despite not having any doubts about Charlie's feelings for me, I still couldn't expect Charlie to want to relocate to a different country so we could be together.

I felt like I could be sick. The thought of not seeing Charlie all the time floored me.

"I don't know," Charlie said. "I mean, I want to be with you, but I guess I hadn't given any thought as to where that would be."

"I know and I'm sorry. You still haven't been given the full brief on what it's like to date a royal."

I lay back on the bed, and Charlie followed me, resting his head on my chest. I ran my fingers through Charlie's red hair.

"Wait, are you going to be king one day?"

"No, Aleksandra is older than me, so she'll be queen once she marries her fiancé, Phillip."

"Oh my god, I forgot there's more of you." Charlie's voice sounded panicked.

"What do you mean?"

"Royal people. How am I going to fit in? I'm only a store manager."

"Hey, hey, look at me." I put my hand on Charlie's chin to tilt his head up. "Everybody is going to love you. You're an amazing person, and you're talented. Do you have any idea how many people will want drawings made by you once they see how stunning your work is?"

"Really?"

"Yes, baby. I might even have to do a royal decree restricting how many hours you can work in the day so I get you to myself."

Charlie chuckled. "I could draw for a living?"

"You won't need to do anything for a living, Charlie, but you can draw for pleasure, and if you want to make a living from it, you can do that too."

Charlie looked like he was considering it.

"How about my family?"

"They will be welcome at the palace any time they want and for as long as they want to stay. There's enough space, that's for sure."

Charlie straddled my hips and kissed me.

"Thank you for thinking of them. I meant that. I wouldn't see much of them. I rarely see them as it is, and I've been promising myself that things would change and I'd go home more often."

"Is there an airport near Chester Falls?"

"Yeah, there's a small one. I don't think it does international flights, though."

"Maybe not, but it'll do private flights. After all, it'll be an honor for the airport to have the prince of Lydovia and his boyfriend use their facilities for their private aircraft."

Charlie's eyes opened wide.

"You have a private jet?"

"I do."

"Man, this is going to take some adjusting."

"I'll be with you every step of the way."

Charlie got up and reached for my hand.

"Come on, we have some regular people stuff to do today, such as attending a regular wedding, and we need a shower."

I laughed.

"Baby, your family is anything but regular. This is going to be the best wedding ever."

"Come on, let's get dirty and clean all in one go," Charlie said, strutting to the bathroom.

I was well on board with that idea too.

---

Hannah looked beautiful as she walked down the aisle toward Ellie, who stood under a wooden arch decorated with purple wisterias. I recognized the look they exchanged as they laced their fingers together in front of the officiant. It was the same look I'd seen in the drawing Charlie had done, and the look I saw in Charlie's eyes every time we were together.

We'd arrived early at the venue so Charlie could present Hannah and Ellie with his wedding gift, a drawing he'd done of two girls holding a book that made the shape of a heart. In true Charlie style, the edges of the girls were slightly blurred so the heart stood out, but there was no mistaking their faces. He'd told me he'd drawn a representation of Hannah and Ellie and how they got together after Ellie started working at Bookmarked.

I put my hand behind Charlie's chair to pull him closer, and he naturally gravitated toward me. The hand he'd placed on my leg would have been a little more dangerous if I hadn't been totally worn out from our pre-shower, during-shower, and post-shower activities. I giggled.

"Why are you giggling like a schoolgirl?" Charlie asked quietly.

"Nothing," I said innocently before stealing a kiss.

Charlie's mom was looking at us adoringly and waved. I missed my mom so much, but I was happy Caroline had enough mom in her to love all her children and their significant halves. I knew that much after the lecture she'd given me right before she'd told me that both James and Sergei were welcome at the wedding too.

Rory sat on the same row of chairs as us. We nodded at each other in acknowledgment. I now saw the underlying sadness in his demeanor. The Rory I'd met initially was an act. I wasn't sure why Rory didn't come out, considering he had such loving and accepting examples all around him.

"Hey," Charlie whispered. "Have you seen how Sergei looks at Rory?"

I had noticed. Sergei had always had a weakness for smaller guys and had complained I wasn't small enough to be thrown around in bed. Who knew, maybe my childhood friend would have his own happy ever after if Rory ever looked up long enough to notice Sergei's eyes on him.

Connor was something else altogether, and I didn't quite know what to make of him. On the surface, he was a confident man who had his life together, despite the Ceecee issues, but there was something else too.

Maybe, like me, Connor had for too long portrayed the role of a perfect human being. It was only a matter of time until one cracked and a new person resurfaced, and my new role in the family was to make sure his younger brother was around enough to be there for him.

After the ceremony, the family and guests were busy taking photos with the brides, so once Charlie and I had had ours taken, Charlie asked me to follow him. We went past the marquee where the reception would be held and kept going until we reached a path.

"Olly told me how to get here," Charlie said as we kept walking until I started to recognize the river. "Remember when we met Aunt Gina that first day? She'd come this way to the lake. The Old Mill is farther down that way." Charlie pointed.

I saw the steps where we'd had our cookies and coffee and…

"That's our tree," Kris said,

"Yes. Come look."

We left the path again toward the tree where we'd given in fully to our attraction for the first time.

"The rain didn't wash everything away," Charlie said with a beaming smile.

"What do you mean?"

I didn't have to wait long to find out because I could see it. There was a circle of seedlings breaking through the soil next to the tree. Inside the circle, there was nothing but soil. That's where we'd sat and scattered the seeds together around our shape as we'd leaned against the tree.

"How is that possible? We only planted them a few days ago."

"The rain. Everything is possible when it rains," Charlie said, and I wholeheartedly agreed.

We stepped into our circle, being careful not to step on top of the seedlings. I leaned against the tree and wrapped my arms around Charlie.

"We have our own made-to-measure spot."

"We do."

I kissed Charlie.

"Kris?"

"Hmm?"

"I never answered your question."

"Which one?"

"About the moving thing."

My heart rate suddenly sped up, and my breathing stopped.

"Yes, I would consider it." Charlie smiled.

"Yes?"

"Yes."

# 24

## CHARLIE

*A YEAR later*

"Babe."

"Hmmm, sleep," I muttered under my breath. I was far too comfortable to wake up.

"Babe."

Strong hands caressed my back until they came around the sides and tickled me until I had no choice but to wake up.

"Fuck you, Kris, I was having a nice dream," I said between giggling like a schoolgirl and trying to escape his torture. "What happened to waking me up with kisses?"

"It didn't work. I've been kissing you for the last

twenty minutes, and you didn't even stir. I was starting to feel like a creep."

To be fair, in the last six months since I'd moved to Lydovia to live with Kris, there wasn't one day I hadn't woken up to kisses and soft touches.

I moved to catch Kris's hands and felt no resistance when I laced our fingers above Kris's head and took his mouth in a hungry morning kiss.

Our erections rubbed against each other, gliding easily with the help of our combined pre-cum.

I straddled Kris and took both our cocks in hand.

"Leave them there." I nodded toward Kris's hands.

"I love it when you take charge," Kris said, pushing his hips up to encourage me to continue stroking us both.

How we even had any energy left was anyone's guess when the reason I was struggling to wake up was because Kris had kept me up late the night before.

"You do, do you?" I teased, applying less pressure now but continuing to stroke us both.

"Fuuuck, Charlie. Please, baby…"

"What do you want?"

"You know what I want," Kris said between short breaths.

"Okay, okay, but only because I'm hungry and breakfast is on you today."

Kris opened his mouth to reply, but after a year together, I knew exactly what to do to bring my prince to climax.

"Do you have any regrets about moving here?" Kris asked while we caressed each other lazily in our post-orgasmic bliss.

"No." And it was the truth. The last year had been such a rollercoaster ride for me, and it hadn't always been easy, but it was definitely worthwhile.

After Hannah and Ellie's wedding when Ceecee's article had come out, my life had changed completely.

I'd attended the president's ball as Kris's plus one. That had been my first exposure to Kris's life as a royal. I'd been terrified, but just as he'd promised, Kris had been there every step of the way.

Going back to work had proved a challenge. Everyone was interested in the department store manager that had stolen the heart of the prince of Lydovia.

After I had lost track of how many times I'd served a customer who'd turned out to be a member of the press trying to interview me, I'd decided I had no option but to quit. Originally, I'd panicked because, without a source of income, I couldn't help Tom pay our rent and bills. That was until Kris had convinced me I didn't need to worry about money.

I hadn't been happy about it, and Tom even less, because when Kris had more or less moved into our apartment, Tom had declared he was allergic to love and went to visit Aunt Gina. After two nights in bed with Kris, I'd been ready to agree to anything.

"Right," Kris said, slapping my bare ass, "up time."

I groaned. I loved spending whole mornings in bed with Kris. Yes, it was indulgent, but after spending six months mostly apart while we'd lived in our respective countries, I just wanted Kris all to myself.

---

When Kris promised an afternoon out doing something fun, the last thing I thought I'd end up doing was hanging halfway down a wall attached to a piece of string attached to a metal bar.

Okay, it wasn't quite like that, but I hadn't gone climbing since that day after I'd met Kris at the Old Mill, and that fear I'd had the first time had returned.

I knew I wouldn't fall and that Kris had made

sure our equipment was safe, but there was something about the possibility of falling that really played on my mind.

"You're doing great, baby. That's it," Kris shouted from the bottom of the wall where he was belaying.

"A picnic would have been nicer," I shouted back.

My legs shook as I struggled to put my weight on them rather than using my hands. I could almost hear Kris's voice in my ear, "*You have more muscles on your legs than on your fingers, use them.*"

"Yes, honey, I am trying, but this is fucking hard," I muttered to myself.

Despite my muscles aching under the unusual strain, once I was past a certain point, I focused on reaching the top. I wasn't going to be defeated by a wall or goddamned gravity.

"You're nearly there, baby," Kris shouted.

I could see the last few moves to the top would be challenging because I didn't see how I could make such a big jump between the holds, but then I remembered how I'd overcome that the first time I'd climbed. I looked around and studied the wall. There were a few good footholds, so all I needed to do was take small steps until I could reach the big handhold at the top.

I took a deep breath and gathered the last bit of

energy I could find, and within seconds, I'd reached the top.

"Wooooooo," I shouted, one hand punching the air in victory.

As I was about to ask Kris to lower me down to the floor, I saw an envelope stuck to the top of the wall. It had my name written on it.

I looked down and saw Kris tightening the rope so I could sit on it safely. It still took a moment until I was confident in releasing both hands from the wall.

I opened the envelope, and inside was a message written in Kris's handwriting.

*My dearest Charlie*

*A year ago, today, and so shortly after we met, you put all your trust in a stranger to keep you safe. You faced the challenge of climbing the wall like you do everything in your life, head-on, plenty of fear, but even more courage.*

*I knew the moment you bumped into me that you were special. There was something about you I couldn't seem to shake off, and I was as attracted to you as a moth is to a flame.*

*You always say I give you too much, but that's not*

*true, my love. You have given me your family, your art, your view of the world, and especially, your heart.*

*Charlie Williams, would you do me the honor of marrying me?*

*Your love always,*
*Kris*

I could barely read the last part of the letter because of the tears in my eyes, and I couldn't even clean them because my hands were dirty with chalk.

I looked down to see Kris on one knee, one hand holding my rope safely and the other holding up a ring box.

All I could do was nod.

Moments later, I was being lowered down. My feet hadn't quite reached the ground when I threw myself at Kris.

"Yes, yes, yes," I said between kisses. "A thousand times yes."

Kris held me tight and spun us around.

"I love you so much, baby," Kris said against my lips.

"I love you too. If only I'd known that to catch a

prince, all I needed was to fall on one," I said, feeling happier than I ever thought was possible. "Now untie me so we can go make out in the shower."

"With pleasure," Kris said as he put one ring on my finger and the other on his own.

I'd never seen Kris move so fast. I could only hope that Kris's private hire of the gym included the showers and changing rooms.

As I held Kris's hand and felt our engagement rings rubbing against each other, I had a vision of our wedding day in the palace gardens with both Kris and my families together, watching us marry under a wooden arch decorated with purple wisteria.

---

Thank you so much for reading How to Catch a Prince, the first book in the Chester Falls series.

Up next is How to Catch a Rival. Follow Tom, Charlie's fashionable best friend who enters, of all things, a bake-off, and finds he's competing against his boss's son, who is equal parts sex-on-legs and emotionless icicle. Follow them as the heat moves from the kitchen to the bedroom and rivalries as momentarily set aside.

Be sure to follow me on Bookbub to be notified

of new releases, and look for me on Facebook for sneak peaks of upcoming stories.

Please take a moment to write a review of How to Catch a Prince. If you leave a review you'll meet a real-life prince within seven days. For real!

If you would like to be the first to know when my new releases are available, read exclusive FREE stories and know what I'm up to, please sign up for my newsletter, Ana's VIP Readers: bit.ly/AnaAshley.

For giveaways, sneak peaks, ARC opportunities and general caffeinated fun times, please join my face-book group! Café RoMMance - Ana's Reader Group

ALSO BY ANA ASHLEY

CHESTER FALLS SERIES

How to Catch a Prince (FREE)

How to Catch a Rival

How to Catch a Bodyguard

How to Catch a Bachelor

How to Catch a Biker

How to Catch a Vet

How to Catch a Happy Ever After

SHORTER STORIES

How to Catch a Bookworm - Short Story

How to Catch the Boss - Novella

CHESTER FALLS IN AUDIOBOOK

Payhip (Most book include an exclusive bonus not available through other retailers)

Apple Store

Google Play

Nook

Kobo

Audible

Chirp

---

FINDING YOU SERIES

Home Again

Together Again

Love Again

Finding You Boxset

with bonus short and extra bonus scenes

---

ROOM FOR 3

The Resort

---

SARINA BOWEN'S WORLD OF TRUE NORTH

Vino & Veritas

Stronghold

## ABOUT ANA

Ana Ashley was born in Portugal but has lived in the United Kingdom for so long, even her friends sometimes doubt if she really is Portuguese.

After getting hooked on reading gay romance, Ana decided to follow her lifelong dream of becoming an author.

These days you can find her in front of her laptop bringing her stories to life, or in the kitchen perfecting her recipe for the famous Portuguese custard tarts.

Ana Ashley writes sweet and steamy gay romance set in America, often in small towns where everyone knows everyone.

---

You can follow Ana on the usual social media hangouts.

For access to exclusive teasers, content, and general book and food related goodness you can now join Ana in her Facebook Group, Café RoMMance - Ana's Reader Group

Ana's VIP Readers - bit.ly/AnaAshley

Facebook Page - @anawritesmm

Email - ana@anaashley.com

Instagram - @anawritesmm

Twitter - @anawritesmm

Bookbub - https://www.bookbub.com/authors/ana-ashley

Goodreads - https://www.goodreads.com/ana-ashley